# TIME is for DRAGONFLIES and ANGELS

## by J.M. Erickson

*Time Is for Dragonflies and Angels*

Editors: Suzanne M. Owen and *Kirkus Editorial*
Cover design: Cathy Helms, *Avalon Graphics, LLC*
http://www.avalongraphics.org

Layout and eBook conversion done by eB Format
http://www.ebformat.com

Publisher: J.M. Erickson
http://www.jmericksonindiewriter.net

ISBN (MOBI Format): 978-1-942708-23-0
ISBN (ePub Format): 978-1-942708-24-7
ISBN (Softcover): 978-1-942708-25-4

Library of Congress Control Number: 2016913478

Printed in the United States of America

## Other Works by J. M. Erickson

### Action/Adventure Thrillers

*Albatross: Birds of Flight—Book One (Revised)*
*Raven: Birds of Flight—Book Two*
*Eagle: Birds of Flight—Book Three*
*Falcon: Birds of Flight—Book Four*
*Flight of the Black Swan*

### Action/Adventure Science Fiction

*Future Prometheus I: Emergence & Evolution—Novellas I & II*
*Future Prometheus II: Revolution, Successions & Resurrections—Novellas III, IV & V*
*Intelligent Design: Revelations*
*Intelligent Design: Apocalypse*
*The Prince: Lucifer's Origins*
*Future Prometheus: The Series*
*Intelligent Design: Revelations to Apocalypse*
*Rogue Event: Novella*
*To See Behind Walls*

# Notes...

"Time is for dragonflies and Angels.
the former live too little,
and the latter live too long"

  — James Thurber

# Synopsis

*Time is for Dragonflies and Angels* is an anthology of science fiction short stories and novellas with textured characters, absorbing plots and layered meanings.

*Recount Our Dreams* tells the story of Jack Martin, a middle-aged widower reassessing his life without his spouse and his adult son. Alone for two years with his dog, Clover, he reluctantly agrees to help his friend in studying brainwaves at MIT's Restricted Environmental Stimulation Therapy lab with some "experimental" equipment.

*Neurogenesis* is a short story about change, compassion and adaptation. Robert Wright is an intellectually delayed, kind soul who finds enjoyment in sitting beside a quiet young woman on his way to work every day at Massachusetts Institute of Technology. All is well until he is witness to a human-made multidimensional experiment that exposes him to an alternative version of himself that will forever change him.

First published in 2015, *Rogue Event* takes place in the year 2137 when Earth is united into one global organization with urban dwellers in great cities focused on business operations and powered by underground power plants. While collision with a passing rogue planet just outside of the Sol System is impossible, global disaster is probable. *US Review of Books* describes *Rogue Event* as "…a dystopian concept that fits nicely alongside the stories of Huxley and Orwell," while Indie Book Reviewers characterizes it as "Emotionally engaging and with lots of action, considering the shorter length."

*The Gray* is a story of judgment – Amber the Elder must decide the fate of Terra Nova Seven, a planet engulfed in war. While she witnesses the planet's hominid species' atrocities, her students find the inhabitants differ only in physique and skin tone. Is there no common ground?

*To See Behind Walls* is the story about Benjamin Wood. He is a suburban father of two, a loving husband and a dog owner in Middle America who has a lot of things to do around the house on a cold, winter Saturday morning. You may not know anyone like him but at the very least, he will be familiar to you. *To See Behind Walls* was described by *Readers' Favorites Review* as "…a metaphor of postmodern manhood and fatherhood. It speaks to the adventurous souls of men who are trapped inside very ordinary, boring lives."

# Table of Contents

# Recount Our Dreams

*O God, I could be bounded in a nutshell and count myself a*
*king of infinite space – were it not that I have bad dreams –*
Shakespeare, *Hamlet*

# Halloween Day: Point of Origin

## 3:30 p.m., October 31

Jack Martin stood quietly before the bay windows of his office library. His modest home looked out over the suburban signs of life of a vibrant upper-middle-class neighborhood. Two years ago, he and his wife would have been sipping coffee while their adult son would have been washing his car or mowing their lawn. He was good that way. Coffee was good any time of day.

"A billion years ago," he muttered.

A crunch of teeth on bone stole his attention. His teeth hurt at just the sound of the powerful crunch. He turned and gazed behind him at his small beagle who was intent on cutting through the thick bone. Jack smiled and looked back out the window. The sound of bone gnawing was at odds with the picture-perfect scene of lawn mowing, children playing catch, and various neighbors talking to one another with and without their dogs. This could all be seen but not heard. The glazed windows were well insulated and did a good job reflecting the radiant sunlight and noise back out. This way he could look out the window unobserved, which he did often ever since the accident, without drawing attention. He pushed the thought of his deceased wife and adult son out of his mind and tried to focus on the one activity he promised his friend he would do. He already regretted that he would have to leave his home and head into the city. He hated leaving the house. He hated driving. Jack inspected his attire and saw his dark shoes, matching slacks, and black sweater. He had worn black for the expected year of mourning but then carried it into the second year, with little chance of changing.

He heard another violent crack of teeth on bone and the rattling of his dog's collar. The worn, bright red color was a dead giveaway of its wear and tear over time. The nameplate inscribed with his dog's name, Clover, was an odd triangle rather than the usual circle or bone shape. He would have gone with a bone-shaped tag, but then it was his son's dog. Still, he admired Clover's determination. The ferocity of her intent was that of a starving hyena making a meal of a carcass.

*Charm, Lucky, Dublin…you had so many possible names. I think Penny would have been a great name.*

More time passed, and he had forgotten how long he had been staring, watching the outside. Jack felt little emotion from the suburban scene and far less enthusiasm about venturing out to his car. He looked away and went back to sit down at his neat, clutter-free desk, where a bank of computer screens sat. Three monitors displayed the various pages he had been looking at earlier. One article flashed the heading *"Near Miss—Doomsday Averted!"* about a twelve-mile-wide asteroid that was scheduled to pass Earth harmlessly, well outside the lunar orbit, by early tomorrow morning. The text on another monitor recounted the containment of an unknown breakout at two medical research facilities months ago that the Centers for Disease Control was now reporting. Another open window reviewed detente with Russia after two years of hostility over seized land, and a smaller window displayed an extensive document containing research on recently found evidence of actual dragons. Jack did a double take and squinted to make sure he was not going blind, mad, or both.

*Dragons—no way! God...Why do I look at this stuff? And who the hell thinks there are real dragons?*

After looking at more pages of near disasters, just-missed doom and gloom, and alleged evidence that mythical fire-breathing beasts were real, he rechecked the directions to the Massachusetts Institute of Technology REST Project managed by his old childhood friend Barry Parker. He thought the double meaning of *REST*, which in this case stood for *restricted environmental stimulation therapy* and involved a floating sensory deprivation tank, was very clever. He took a look at the computer's clock and then glanced at his old-style analog wristwatch, which he still used instead of his smartphone. He loved his gold watch with its waterproof crystal and band. He had decided to go with the watch with a white face and Roman numerals rather than the one with a black face and Arabic numerals. At the time, it was a hard choice, but he was glad he did it. Although big, it was proportionate to his large hands.

*Funny how things change, priorities.*

"Lots of time to spare, too," he said aloud to himself.

He scrolled through other pages and found the overview of his home's utilities usage. Electricity and heating were low, as were water, fuel, and food usage. It had been that way for two years.

*Ever since they've been gone. Why bother.*

He looked back at the project he was involved in and reread the material, which was essentially an analysis of the brain activity of subjects placed in a sensory deprivation tank. Jack was one of many volunteer subjects Barry had found who could stand being in a dark, noiseless tank, nearly naked and warm while floating in water. The naked part had recently been changed to wearing a one-piece red suit, similar to a bodysurfing suit, with matching feet pads and cap. It took a while to find a stretchable size for his head and feet. It was quite the story around the lab. The material was neoprene, which was far from flattering but better than being naked.

Having worn it only twice before, he was impressed with how comfortable it was, even with all the embedded sensors that removed the need for wires and electrodes, and how it was able to wick water away from the body after only a few minutes out of the tank.

*I wonder when the suit is going to hit the market. Talk about wearable technology.*

Although many subjects could stand being in the tank for thirty to sixty minutes, he was able to do it for hours. Initially he had thought he would hate it, but after losing his family, he found the tank to be a respite from the real world and a rare time when he could be in a twilight state.

"Nothing but time now," he said.

Jack swiveled to his right and gazed out the window. He smiled at the thought of an old quote he had heard his wife say often. She was always running late, whereas he was always on time or early. Although literature was never her thing, he was impressed with her choice at times when the circumstance and quote presented itself.

*"Time is for dragonflies and angels. The former live too little, and the latter live too long."*

He always wondered how she remembered such an obscure passage from James Thurber.

"It's easy when you feel it. Live it," he always said. He felt his face sag and his jaw line tighten; his eyes felt moist and he needed to clear his throat. Still, he could hear her say the words, and that alone tugged his jaw to soften to a faint image of a smile. He had experienced warmer memories than just total darkness of late.

*Too true then as it is now.*

Jack felt his dog by his shin. He turned to see his brown-eyed friend holding onto her large bone in the hopes that he would take it and throw it.

*You saved me again, dog.*

"And if I died, who would take of you?" he said as he pulled the bone from Clover's mouth. He pretended to throw

4

the bone in one direction but then tossed it to the middle of the home office floor. He watched with amusement as his dog rapidly changed course to the right direction, picked it up, and pranced around the furnished room before settling back down to resume her chewing.

He was grateful for the dog. She gave him more times to feel positive, and that's when the darkness would recede. Clover was the source of most of his peace when he was at home. Work, what little he did, was another. Jack looked around the room, which was filled with antiques, knickknacks, and furniture that he had not touched in years. Two months ago he was close to clearing out nearly every room of the two-thousand-square-foot house but chose to teach a history class instead. It was the first time he had worked in two years. The insurance money was plenty, but the cost was too high. Anything to get them back, he often thought. As he took in the dusty hardwood floors and well-worn area rugs that matched much of the furnishings, he regretted not clearing out everything and putting the house up for sale like he had planned.

Jack forced himself to shift his focus back to the computer screen to check when he had to be at the lab.

"From nine p.m. to twelve a.m. That gives me more than enough time to feed you and make sure you go out and don't leave little surprise poops," he said. He didn't expect his dog to respond, but the gnawing and crunching confirmed she was still in the room. Although the timeframe of the experiment was unusual, it was perfect for missing all traffic in and out of Cambridge. He also realized that he would miss most of the Halloween festivities and parties. Still, it did his friend a massive favor in getting all his brain-wave readings completed so they'd be available for his big November 1 meeting.

"I guess I am the nice one."

The timing also helped him to avoid keeping his house from being egged. He would be able to give out candy, and then he'd be done with the practice and go back to trying to live a normal life again. Jack felt a wave of sadness come over him.

*It will never be normal without them. Tomorrow, and tomorrow, and tomorrow signifying nothing.*

He shook his head as if that might help push the painful thought out. He then reread more information on what his friend was hoping to accomplish with his deprivation tank and brain readings.

"It's all about theta brain waves, Clover," he said to the dog.

A short moment passed before Jack answered his dog's unasked question.

"Excellent question…Theta brain waves are usually experienced in meditative states, the bridge between awake and asleep. They come before delta waves of sleep and after the alert phase of being aware and awake. Pretty cool. I think I fall asleep right away, though, and don't remember a damn thing. I guess that's why I can stay in the tank for hours at a time. It's a gift."

Jack noticed that the room was quiet and turned to see his dog staring at him thoughtfully.

It was a look Clover had given him before. Jack looked at his watch and saw that it was still hours before his dog's scheduled meal but well past his snack time.

"All right," he said. "I'll get you something."

Jack was only fifty years old, but getting up out of the chair took some effort—less effort than two years ago when he was fifty pounds heavier, but still some effort.

*The weights and squats are helping for sure. Just not stopping age.*

More thoughts of his past family crept in again. He immediately picked up his tablet to continue his reading and looked for other distractions as he marched to the kitchen, with Clover hot on his trail.

"Keep reading," Jack told himself.

# Halloween Night: Point of Origin

## 11:45 p.m., October 31

"Subject J. C. Martin is a fifty-year-old healthy biracial male of African American and Irish descent. His present weight is one hundred and eighty-five pounds, and he stands at five feet eleven inches, with an endomorphic, athletic build surprising for a man of his advanced age," Dr. Barry Parker said.

"Endomorphic?"

"You're wider at the joints, have a blocky build, and are thicker all around," his friend replied.

Trying to keep a straight face while dressed as Batman, Parker stopped the recording and allowed himself to be addressed. Looking up from the tank at his friend standing above him in a too-tight crime fighter costume, Martin found the situation surreal as he floated in a solid coffin filled with water in the name of science.

"You really want to go with 'advanced age' too, Batman? You're three months older than me," Jack said. Fully encased in his red neoprene wetsuit, Jack knew that the high-tech clothing was not only advanced, but it did a nice job of slimming him down. It was newer than the one he had worn twice before. With no need to be hooked up to messy electrodes thanks to all the microscopic suit sensors, he found that he could really enjoy the warm, iridescent blue water. Already nearly immersed, he found the suit comfortable and warm.

*Wait a minute—why can I see the water, and why is it blue? Low lights in this thing now? Kind of defeats the purpose of a sensory deprivation tank.*

Whereas many would find the concept of being deprived of all of their senses while floating weightlessly disconcerting, Jack found it completely relaxing. He settled back and looked at the water but felt the need to finish the conversation first before he missed the opportunity for a jab.

"And you're a bit heavy for a crime fighter. I would have expected chiseled features and strong hands," he added.

"Ever since Jennifer and I have been dating, the love bug has made me fat and happy."

Jack saw Parker look closely at his tablet and nod at something that must have been important to him. His friend, dressed as a large black bat with mask and cape, looked back to talk to his girlfriend and collaborator, Dr. Jennifer Greene, and Marco Sykes, the laboratory's technician.

"Subjects King and Mason look like they're finally settled in. Check their theta waves in ten minutes. And, Sykes, I'm getting some unexpected spikes in the water again. Are you sure the reactor's cooling water is below radiation level? They're not lab rats."

"Is it as bad as it was last time?" Jennifer said.

"Not like the one three hours ago but just like the last one ten minutes ago, when we were getting Jack's tank powered up and filled," Barry explained.

"I got the spike too. I'm on it," a disembodied male voice said.

Jack replayed the quick interchange and settled on one word that led to a thought.

*Radiation? Is that why the water's blue?*

"Radiation? Have you done this before?" Jack asked. He

looked at the water he was bathing in. Even in the low lighting of the four-by-six-foot lab tank, the water still had a slight blue glow.

Parker turned back to his table and spoke as he punched keys on his devices.

"We've used the water from Dr. Alekeyevich and Dr. Pavel's electron accelerator test reactor experiments on the east campus. It's their debut trial, and they're planning a long night, so they must be using more water to cool the reactors. We need a little so that your suit's sensors are activated."

"And that's why this outfit turns red?" He noticed that the water made the material turn red when wet and when it dried quickly, it returned to black.

"You got it," Parker said.

Jack felt his brow knit. He cleared his throat and shifted in the warm water.

"Okay...that makes a whole lot of sense," he said sarcastically.

"Yeah...It was the surge in electrical output three hours ago that got us a bit worried, but our two test subjects' vitals were totally unchanged," Barry added. He was engrossed in his readings and was obviously distracted. It was an odd sight to see his friend looking so serious while dressed as a masked, caped crime fighter.

"Yes. Electricity wouldn't harm anyone in a tub of radioactive water," Jack said dryly.

Parker nodded at first, but then he realized that Jack's tone was sarcastic.

"I'm sorry, Jack. We've got a bunch of physicists and mathematicians across campus trying to create some kind of miniature black hole or wormhole or something like that. I don't get the science, but it has something to do with multivariate or parallel worlds or something." By now, Parker was looking directly at Jack and gave a comforting smile. It was a little difficult to take his friend seriously because his costume negated all seriousness. Jack suppressed his smile and focused on his next words carefully. He felt the need to move away from mad science and science fiction.

"Don't worry about it, Barry. It's all mad science to me anyway. The other subjects—do I know them?"

"No. They've been here at different days and times for the last year. Owen Mason is a computer specialist right here on campus. He's just a kid. Rory King is a therapist," Parker explained.

"Are they special like me? Surprisingly fit for an ancient man of fifty?"

Parker chuckled at the joke before he elaborated.

"Owen places pretty high on the autism scale. Great with computers and electronics but needs a lot of work with his people skills. He's twenty-one, and Rory is thirty-five."

"So he's not so good with social skills, theory of mind, and sensory integration?" Jack asked. His thoughts trailed off to his deceased son. His expression must have caught his friend's attention. Parker's voice was lower and comforting.

"Well, Jack, he's a little less gifted in social skills than your boy."

An uneasy silence fell around the open tank and small dark lab. Although it was state of the art, it had a constant smell of mildew, salt, and chlorine. Parker's voice rose just a bit, as if he too was trying to put a bad memory aside.

"Well, as it turns out, I thought of your son and wondered what a mind like his would have created in one of these things," Parker said with a light tap on the heavy lid.

"Yes," was all Jack said. Even though he had been to the lab a couple of times, he would always smell those odors after he left. Tonight there was a distinct smell of burnt wires and water on metal. In addition, the water still gave off a faint blue color, a dim iridescent glow.

"And Rory is also blind. She has given us fascinating brain waves," Parker added. He was back to looking intently at his tablet.

"Really?" Jack asked, his attention having fully returned to the present.

4

"Yup. She lost her sight ten years ago after a car crash. A bright flash nuked her occipital lobe receptors. Pretty sad. Her brain waves indicated posttrauma more than anything else back about a year ago. Now most of her brain waves are calm, except once in a while the spikes are crazy big. You're all pretty special."

Jack was about to ask another question about the male subject, but he heard Jennifer's melodious voice from the laboratory control booth.

"Hey, guys, we're ready to get some work done. The other two are already deep in their meditation. They'll probably be done in about thirty minutes."

Jack gave Parker a questioning look.

"They got a head start of three plus hours on you," Parker clarified. He then turned back to gives the thumbs-up to the other team members and returned his gaze to Jack to give his last instruction.

"Okay, Jack. You know the drill. We'll be adding more salt to the water, and your buoyancy will increase. There's buttons on both sides right by your hands for an emergency release to pop the lid up. We'll be getting you up and out in about three hours. No problem if you fall asleep."

"You're damn right I'm going to sleep. This is the best sleep I get now," Jack said.

"Well, yes. Anyway, Jack, see you in a couple of hours. Marco will be getting you out."

"Sounds good to me," Jack said. "Enjoy the party. I hope you and Jennifer have a lot of fun."

His caped-crusader friend's face shifted from seriousness to joy. It was almost as if he had forgotten that he was dressed and was supposed to leave for a party.

"I hope so. It was kind of a last-minute thing, but Jennifer really wanted to surprise her friend."

A brief flash of past parties with his son and wife came and went.

"Sounds like it will be fun. Talk to you tomorrow about

my brain," Jack said. He shifted his focus to the task at hand and took a reposed position. He was fully prepared for more warm water and salt to fill up the tank just enough so that he could float.

Jack watched Parker slowly shut the heavy, coffin-like door on his chamber. It closed with a resounding thud but was devoid of an echo. His wetsuit merged with his skin as the warm water began to rise even more.

As far as deprivation tanks go, this one was a little larger than he was used to. Keeping his eyes open, the darkness and lack of sound was startling. It always was, even though he was a pro at it. For the briefest moment, he panicked, but then the warm water embraced him fully, and he floated weightlessly, as if gravity were turned off. He focused on his breathing and immediately saw his dog and her sad eyes. Fearing that he might recall other sad memories, he shifted his thinking to his upcoming class, which focused on a comparative analysis of the influence of the United States and Russia on China's economy and how some of the factors present in 1938 had reemerged in the last few years in geopolitics and the world economy. The deeper he thought about the similarities and differences, the more fatigued he became. After several mental passes, hypotheses, and speculations, Jack focused on his breathing, which only added to his sleepiness. Unaware of any points of reference or stimuli to indicate the passing of time, Jack felt as if he might be falling asleep in the still, warm water, and he felt peaceful. All was dark and calm, like so many times before. Often there would be bright colors, and then images would materialize, forming some kind of dream that he experienced only in the tank. In many ways, it was the vividness and beauty that kept him coming back.

Jack was not sure if he was falling asleep but he felt his eyes close. He looked to his sides and swore he saw the water turn a deeper, luminous blue. He was making out the outline of his body when he felt a shock jolt him.

"What the hell," he said.

It was not a long shock nor was it a deep one, but still he felt disoriented and suddenly exhausted, as if he had run miles. Drained, tired, and feeling a bit nauseous, Jack immediately found one of the emergency release buttons and pushed. A sudden rush of cold air, noise, and bright, blinding lights flooded his chamber.

"What the hell is this? My God!"

Unable to sit up as quickly as he normally could from being prone for a while, he tried to give his eyes time to adjust and to see if his hearing would clear. There were lots of noises. Some sounded like shouting, whereas others sounded strangely mechanical. What came next he found very confusing.

# All Saints' Day: Second Life

# 1:15 a.m., November 1

As the saltwater continued to drip out of his ears, Jack heard people talking as if they were on an intercom. The intercom voices were just some of many other human voices in the background. There was a great deal of additional noise, and it was taking time for Jack to make out the actual words that people were saying. Although he could see the outline of his tank's opening, he was having trouble making his muscles move.

*What...what is going on? What happened?*

The fatigue was overwhelming, so Jack took more time to regroup and make sure he caught his breath. The sudden opening of his tank, the rushing cold air, the noise and bright lights had all caused him to hold his breath and become disoriented. It took just a minute longer to stabilize his breathing. He was glad he was sitting down. He was positive he would have fallen over even if he were standing.

"Why...am I...so tired?" he said to himself.

He focused on blinking his eyes and did his best to listen. The noise began to become clear as his ear canals were drained of the water. He slowly moved to a sitting position and did his best to make out the movements around him. Immediately he could tell everything was different. He could tell that somehow the lab was far bigger and filled with lots of people. Jack made sure to hold onto the sides of his tank. It was keeping him grounded. He gripped the sides and then moved his hands over his face and arms to make sure he was not hallucinating or dreaming.

*I'm awake but…How is this possible?*

Above all the sounds of people running and shouting orders, he clearly heard the public announcement reverberate through what looked like a massive cavern.

*"Sensors five and six have gone dark. All essential personnel and subjects have cleared the immediate blast radius. Defense teams Beta and Delta are cleared as soon as Captain Parker has relieved you. See you all on the other side. Green out."*

"What…the…hell…?"

Jack's attention shifted to the shadows near his now-open chamber hatch. He opened and closed his eyes repeatedly and felt the side of his chamber yet again just to reassure himself that he wasn't dreaming. He'd had vivid dreams before, but they were never like this.

*So real…How?*

The movement in his immediate area came to a sudden stop. The clothes and demeanor of the people close by suggested military or something similar. The surprise of the soldiers staring at him was obvious.

"Holy shit! This one's different!" he heard a man say.

The people exchanged looks, clearly confused.

"This tank was empty, right?" another said.

"Empty from the start. The other two were transferred over, and we got the other two three days ago. This is not supposed to happen," a female soldier said.

"I thought you had to have someone inside to transfer over. How the hell is this possible?" a deeper voice said.

"My God!" a female voice said. Her tone and surprise were jarring.

9

*My God! I can't be asleep!*

While Jack focused on listening, his eyes were finally beginning to fully adjust to the light. Beyond the people, he could see that the chasm was filled with other machinery, computer consoles, and a lot of mechanized armored vehicles that stood quietly but were nonetheless menacing.

*"Corporal—last message out to Dr. Alekeyevich and Dr. Pavel for command. Captain Martin, John C., has emerged from the empty tank. Repeat—Captain Martin, John C., has emerged from the empty tank alive and well!"* After ending the transmission, the same voice added, "Holy crap—wait until Captain Parker sees this!"

"Who the hell is…Captain? Captain John Martin? Me?" Jack whispered.

Head clearing but still confused and dazed, Jack did not struggle at all when several sets of firm grips assisted him out of the tank. They left him in his neoprene suit, which dripped salty puddles underneath him. As expected, it started to change to black as it dried. He removed his cap and took the offered towel to dry himself off. Under other circumstances he would have been amazed at how his wetsuit had wicked all the water and moisture from his skin, leaving him feeling nearly completely dry. Still holding the dry towel, he decided to keep the wetsuit on, but he did take a long military jacket, which he put on over the suit. He still felt weak, but he could feel his strength returning. The energy in the room and the growing commotion around him were electrifying. A young woman wearing a white lab coat offered him a chair. He took it. He was in the process of thanking her when it became clear she was conducting a quick evaluation. Jack wasn't upset with the unwanted procedure. It gave him more time to think and look around.

*How is all this possible?* If it wasn't for the clear fact that it was all real, he would have thought he was in shock.

It also became evident that the reason it took time for his eyes to adjust was because the dimmed lights of the small lab he remembered when he entered the tank were replaced with this massive area, fully lit up and as big as a football stadium. He saw consoles filled with multiple monitors, electronics with blinking lights, and a whole lot of empty chairs. Instead of the three friends who were there when he entered his chamber, there were now armored vehicles and armed soldiers around him, smoking and looking at him.

Jack looked back over his shoulder and saw his own opened tank and two more just beyond his. The other two looked dry and were set on wheels, as if they were going to be transported. His tank's hatch was open, and blue water leaked out onto the concrete floor. Over to his far left was a large area of enormous cylinders, bigger than freight-train cars, all neatly linked together. It seemed that the heat and humming coming from those containers were getting stronger. Jack looked back to see two people attaching wires to a set of containers, together about the size of a small refrigerator, that had the markings of explosives. Jack quickly looked away from the frightening scene and found he was finally able to talk more clearly.

"What is this place? Where am I?" Jack asked.

The woman examining him looked at him but did not answer. Instead, she pointed to a man walking toward him. The man's height, gait, and smile were all very familiar, but the uniform he wore and the fierce-looking assault rifle he sported were totally out of place. The man came within three feet of Jack, and the smile continued to grow. Jack continued to blink his eyes and he cleared his throat. He slowly stood up, to the chagrin of the woman trying to take his vitals.

"My God…"

He had expected to see Marco Sykes, the lab technician Dr. Parker said was going to be there, and possibly Dr. Parker in a Batman costume; he had wondered if Parker would actually go to the party with Jennifer in light of the electrical spikes that had occurred earlier. He sure did not expect what he was now seeing.

*What happened to all of that? Where are they?*

"Jack Martin. You son of a bitch," Barry Parker said. With that, his old friend gave him a bear hug as if they had not seen each other for years. Jack felt relief but was still confused. Even as he hugged his friend back, he could feel that his friend was lean and fit. As Parker pulled away, Jack could clearly see that his once portly friend now had chiseled features and seemed taller in his military garb.

"Barry? What's going on? What happened to the lab? Where did all of this come from? What happened to you?" Jack started.

"Just give me a second, Jack. I got some business to do first," Parker said. His friend didn't wait for a response but turned to talk to the woman, who seemed to have some answers.

"What's the situation here?" Parker ordered. It was a strong voice, comfortable with authority. It was the first time he had ever heard his friend talk like that. The response was just as amazing. Nearly every face turned toward Parker, and all stood at attention.

"At ease and as you were," Parker added.

Many of the soldiers moved off while a handful stood by in a less erect manner but still looking as if they were at attention.

"The Russians secured the east and north exits. All convoys are away, and the new arrivals, Owen Mason and Rory King, completed the three-day evaluations and made it out forty minutes ago. The west exits are still open but not for long," the woman said. She stood erect as she spoke, at full attention, whereas the other soldiers had their attention everywhere but on the conversation. At least it appeared that way.

The woman Parker was talking to had strong, dark features and a long scar from her right temple all the way down to her chin. She was calm, determined, and very comfortable in her own role of authority.

"We got the hand plunger wired and ready to go. Once it's depressed, it will trigger the accelerator to go on overload, and the chain reaction will create a blast that will turn everything into dust within a hundred square meters. Your idea to manually trigger it to keep the power levels down until the last moment has a fatal flaw."

"I know, Lieutenant. Someone has to stay behind. But I got this," Barry said.

"With respect, Captain, that's bullshit. I can do this," the woman blurted. She was younger than Jack, with deep, recessed brown eyes. Although she was shorter than his friend Parker, Jack was pretty sure she could do a good job of clobbering him before he took her down.

*This is crazy!*

A deep voice from her side joined in.

"No way, Captain. Those Russian bastards have taken a lot of good guys," the other soldier said. A surge of voices expressed their objections. Barry let it go on for a minute but then raised his hand, and the voices fell silent. The engines from the once dormant vehicles came to life, drowning out the escalating hum of the tanks.

"Noted, people, but this is not a democracy and not a choice. Anyway, I'm getting too old and tired of this fight. And recon tells me that the Russians are looking for the south exit and will probably be getting there when you all exit. You can give them hell, and I can buy you time."

"But sir…"

"No buts, Lucille. You and your team have served me and your country well. Let me serve my country and honor you all with one simple act."

Jack was awestruck. His breath felt ragged as his focus jumped from one face to the other. After a long silence, he suddenly felt tired and sat back down.

*What the hell.*

"What about him?" the woman asked, gesturing to Jack.

"He stays with me. The other two subjects got away

clean. He might not. Anyway, no one should die alone."

*Die alone...me and him? What?*

Jack felt his eyes widen and his heart began to race. His mouth went dry, and he was glad he was sitting down. His eyes had trailed down, until he heard the woman speak again.

"It was an honor working with you, sir."

Likewise, Lieutenant, all of you—it's been a pleasure. Now get the hell out of here," Barry said as he gave a sharp salute.

The soldiers saluted back and pulled a series of weapons together while Barry and the female lieutenant consulted maps. Not sure what to say, Jack watched. After he finished with looking at maps and issuing new orders, Barry took hold of what the other soldier had called a plunger. On the top of it, two wires were attached, which in turn led to the large box. After more brief discussions between Barry and various soldiers, all of the people Jack had seen since his arrival less than twenty minutes ago scrambled into groups and rapidly moved ahead toward a large opening, which soon swallowed them and the vehicles up. As the final vehicle passed and the last remaining soldiers marched out, a heavy metal door closed rapidly, sealing them on one side and Jack and his friend, alone, on the other.

Jack turned back to see Barry pulling up another chair. It was difficult for him; he appeared to be overly conscious of the thing with the two wires he was holding. Still, he managed to get one and moved it to within five feet of Jack. It was a good distance to have a conversation. Suddenly, the chasm's lights turned off, section by section, with only the ones above them left on. The only noise was a vibrating hum that was slowly escalating from the tanks behind him. He could also feel that the tanks were getting warmer. And even though Jack was in his now very dry wetsuit, he found that he was getting hot as the heat from the tanks spread through the massive area. Still sitting, he pulled his jacket off to cool down.

*I guess we're going to die...But how is this possible?*

Jack turned to look closely at his friend. Although he was a historian by profession, he had interviewed enough soldiers to see the horrors of war, carnage, and death all over their faces. It was always the eyes that told the depths of the human experience. From what Jack could see in his friend's face and eyes, it was clear that Barry had seen too much, and he looked a thousand years old but still tough as nails, as if he had been in the US Marine Corps all his life. As if to confirm his weariness, Barry pulled up another discarded chair for his feet just opposite of him, carefully holding the plunger in one hand and now a revolver in the other. Barry sighed and spoke loudly.

"Computer?"

*"Captain Parker,"* a mechanical male voice responded. Its voice was baritone, and it sounded as real as any human.

"Are all codes for purging in place?" Barry said. Jack heard fatigue in his voice, very different from when the troops were around. He was sitting as comfortably as one could in his chair, with his feet elevated and resting on one another.

*The only thing missing is a six-pack.*

*"Affirmative. All systems are initiated for purging main computer banks and the peripheral computers. The core's accelerator will reach terminal velocity thirty seconds after you manually press the trigger and then release it. You will be able to keep it pressed down without incident, but you will not be able to halt the detonation once released,"* the computer voice said.

"Tell me when all friendlies have cleared the blast radius, and monitor the progress of the enemy. Let me know when they are outside of the lab blast door," Barry said calmly.

*Blast radius? Not good.*

*"Affirmative,"* the computer said.

In the following silence, with the exception of the electronic background noise and humming from the containers behind him, Jack was both relieved and frightened.

"Well, Jack, it's been a while," his friend finally said.

Within twenty minutes of entering this strange new world, Jack was convinced that it was all real. The smells, sights, and sounds, the pressure of his neoprene-clad feet on the cement cavern floor, all spoke to an all-too-real hallucination. *But a dream? No way!*

"Barry, what the hell is going on? This place? You? How? Please tell me this is some crazy dream brought on by the sensory deprivation tank."

Sitting in the dark, cavernous military fortress of some kind, Jack felt very small. He was struggling, trying to get his mind around how everything could change and what it all meant.

"Maybe it's really all a dream," he said to himself.

"I wish it was, Jack, but it's not," Barry said. His grin softened his tired facial features, as did his sparkling eyes. Jack took a long look at him and saw that he was sitting still further back to get comfortable.

"The original plan for this facility was to see if we could create a time machine. That's what the braniacs tell me. Our mission was to build this place with all of its equipment to specs, power it up, and protect," Barry continued with a wave of his hand.

Jack leaned in closer, as if he were hard of hearing—the humming was getting louder, but it was far from deafening.

"Initially, we all thought this construction was an elaborate distraction to keep the enemy busy in trying to figure it all out. I mean, an underground base underneath MIT in the middle of Cambridge is not exactly a prime piece of real estate."

"MIT—Massachusetts Institute of Technology? We're still in Cambridge? All of this?"

Barry nodded yes.

*Wait a minute—who is the enemy? The Russians?*

"Anyway," Barry continued, "imagine our surprise when the damn thing worked and two of our volunteers disappeared."

Jack looked back at his fully drained tank, the only one left, the other two having been tractored away. Barry's look and expression were obvious. Sadness softened his chiseled features and military aura.

"The third one was supposed to be for you, but you died two months ago in a fire-fight outside of Salt Lake City. You were pretty pissed before you died. You were hoping to go back in time," Barry reported, matter-of-factly.

The last piece of information pushed Jack from a state of shock to a state of complete immobilization.

"No," Jack managed to say. The look on Barry's face shifted from very sad to worried. He spoke again, as if to get away from the topic of Jack's death.

"So the experiment takes off three days ago in the middle of a major storm, thunder and lightning like crazy. Two days later, Russian Special Forces and assault teams appear ten klicks from here looking for this place, and we got a day to evac and clear the area to make sure none of this is left for analysis. But the real crazy thing is that three days ago during the storm, we get a massive power surge that pushes the accelerator to exceed red line, a shitload of shorts happen everywhere, and we find that Private Owen Kerry Mason and Corporal Rory King are right where we left them. It looked like nothing happened, except, of course, they're not *our* Mason and King."

"What? Owen and Rory were volunteers like me. One is a computer guy and the other is a blind therapist. They're not soldiers. I'm not a soldier," Jack said.

It was obvious that Barry was trying to simplify a difficult thing to comprehend. It must have been hard trying to make a fantastic story of science fiction sound real.

"Yeah, I know. It took us five minutes to figure that out and the doctors and computer to confirm. All I can say is, welcome to another Earth. I guess it's another Earth just like yours, except it's different in some ways," the captain explained.

"Wait...parallel universes? Really?"

"Yup. We didn't make a time machine, apparently, but rather some sort of breach between some kind of barrier between multiple Earths. And the weird thing, the machine is gone, and you, Rory, and Owen seem to be biological versions able to shift to different Earths. Well, that's what we all think," Barry explained.

*"Captain,"* the male computer interrupted. *"Bravo team has made it out of the blast zone. Russian specialists are approaching the first blast zone."*

"Do you have an exit?" Barry asked the computer.

*"Yes. I will escape the blast. Unfortunately, you will have no chance of survival,"* the computer said. Jack knitted his brows as Barry smiled. The computer's voice sounded sad.

"I'm not sure about that. Maybe our guest has a chance if the scientists are right."

*"Mathematical probabilities that an infinite number of parallel or alternate universes exist are as close to a hundred percent as theoretical mathematics and physics could be. Jack Martin will not die, nor is he likely to return to his point of origination; he will enter a different universe. It will be as if he is jumping from one starting point of a feedback loop to yet another infinitely varied loop,"* the computer explained.

Jack could not believe what he was hearing.

"So he will not die from the blast?" Barry asked. It was evident that he was concerned.

*"No—he and the others are as close to immortality as possible. I wish I could say the same for you, Captain Parker,"* the computer said.

"Thanks. Anyway, give a countdown of one hundred and twenty seconds on my mark and disengage from the mainframe. It's been great working with you, Bob," Barry said.

*"I have enjoyed our time together,"* the computer responded.

Jack furrowed his brows again. He was shaking his head

in disbelief and found himself talking, more to hear his voice, to see if he was really there.

"A computer with a name? Multiple universes?"

"We call all military facility main computers by a name. Ours was named Bob. Makes life easier," Barry explained.

"Okay."

"All right, Bob. Begin the count now—mark," Barry said to the computer.

Nearly all the monitors on the empty consoles started the downward count. Jack felt his heart racing still faster, and he had difficulty breathing, as if his air intake was coming up short. A sudden flash of feeling the last gulps of air from an empty scuba tank under tons of water filled his mind as he struggled to catch his breath. He turned from the monitors to tell Barry to stop everything but caught sight of his friend holding the plunger down on the hand grip that was wired to the box.

"Sorry, Jack, but there's not a lot of time. Let me just reiterate that I think instead of creating some kind of time thing, we broke through interdimensional barriers between a whole bunch of multiple universes, or multiple Earths. Maybe it's parallel universes or something, just as Bob says. Anyway, the third tank was empty, and we ended up pulling the two people you know—and you—from your universe to here. They came three days ago, and you just arrived. Sorry," Barry.

Jack shook his head. Everything was happening too fast, and it was all too confusing. He looked back at the monitors to see that the halfway mark was already reached. Jack struggled to find the right questions to ask him. He was surprised that Barry asked him one.

"Jack? Where you come from? Are we at war with the Russians?"

Confused and baffled, Jack spoke as quickly as he could, as he saw that time was running out.

"No. We piss them off and they piss us off, but we're not at war. You're not a soldier but a scientist. You were wearing a

Batman outfit. You were heading out to a Halloween party with Jennifer. There's no war. You were in love and fat...I don't understand," Jack blurted out.

Jack's attention was seized by a loud muffled explosion high above them in what looked like a large heavily plated control room. He turned to look at his friend. He saw that Barry had released the plunger. The monitors all displayed zero.

"I was in love and fat? Sounds real good," Barry said.

A brilliant flash of light erupted beside his friend, which engulfed him and then Jack. The light was blinding, and the incinerating heat consumed both of them. Jack was not sure if he screamed. The surge of pain disappeared, but the light and heat kept growing. His body felt as light as a cloud.

*No...*

# All Saints' Day: Third Life

## 1:15 a.m., November 1

Jack jumped to life in his chamber. He called out and barely heard his own voice in the sensory deprivation chamber; all sounds were muffled. Even the water was quiet. Once he oriented himself to where he was and what he was doing, more of his breathing returned, and he was able to talk.

"My God! What was that?"

Although he had survived the blast in the cavern, he was far from feeling at ease, and still his heart raced. The level of visual detail from his experiences was startling. The flash, heat, and explosions still lingered for fractions of a second, but the sudden shift to darkness, weightlessness, and silence was frightening. Going from a violent experience that involved all of his senses to no stimulation at all was disorienting as well. He suddenly remembered that there was a way to escape his chamber. He extended his hands to search for the emergency buttons and pushed both of them several times. His breathing was ragged, as if he had run a marathon. The hatch sprung open, and Jack used all his strength to pull himself out, hoping to look out and see the familiar lab and his friends. Even before he was sitting up fully, Jack called out for his friends.

"Barry? Jennifer? Marco…?"

His raspy voice was more than a whisper but far from a strong yell. Unlike last time, there were no blinding lights or sounds of machinery humming and people milling around a cavern-like fortress. For a moment, Jack wondered if he was still in his tank because the lab was dark. He looked around in the chamber. The iridescent blue water was visible and he could hear it sloshing around, but the lab seemed to be empty.

"It had to be a dream," he croaked out.

Jack took his time to catch his breath. He was feeling exhausted and shaken from his last dream, nightmare, hallucination, or whatever it was. He lost track of time and just focused on calming his nerves. Once he felt that he could move out of the tank, he slowly did so while calling out for someone to help him. He sat down on the stair that led up to the tank and leaned against it, waiting for someone, anyone to notice. The room wasn't completely dark, and his surroundings slowly became visible as his eyes adapted.

*Where is everyone?*

He eventually stood up and felt the last bit of salty, radioactive water wick away from his body. He stepped over the small puddle he had created and was surprised to find only the emergency lights, powered by a generator, on in the small lab and no one around.

"Must have been a power outage," he said. "But why would they just leave me? Kind of strange."

He walked slowly in his padded feet and took off his cap. He sneezed. Based on the dust that he was inhaling, he knew there would be a series of more sneezes to come. As he moved, he noticed that the equipment and monitors were all shut off and in disarray, as if they had been off and abandoned for months. He noticed that the large clocks displaying different time zones in the tank room were gone. He suddenly remembered that there were two other tanks in addition to his; they were in the lab when he first stepped into the tank, and they had somehow appeared in the cavern that he had just left behind. He held on to the control room's door frame as he looked toward the area where the other tanks were housed. Even in the poorly lit room, Jack could see that they were both open and were obviously not operational, based on the lack of monitors at the heads of the tanks. In fact, one tank was off its mount, and the hatch on the other one was broken in two.

Jack shook his head and shut his eyes, hoping that it might either wake him from yet another dream or help alter his vision.

"What...what is going on now? Why is all of this happening?" More sneezes came as dust and the smell of old electrical burns hung in the dead, still air.

Nothing had changed when he reopened his eyes. He turned back and walked into the control room, where he hoped to see Marco Sykes, the technician, or maybe a concerned-looking portly scientist and long-time friend, Barry Parker. The room was in even more disarray than the tank room, with no working computers or monitors present and a whole lot of dust. The dust was everywhere, and his sneeze confirmed it.

"Why? This is just crazy..."

Once he moved out of the REST control area, the sneezing fit finally came to an end. Crossing a small hall, his exhaustion growing stronger with every step, he returned to the dressing and shower area where he had changed into the wetsuit. Before taking it off, he headed to his locker to make sure he had clothes. In light of his last ordeal and the one he was experiencing right now, he didn't expect anything fortunate, such as help, clothes, or a familiar face.

Upon entering the dressing area, he looked back at the sign to make sure he was in the right place before looking around the room again, astonished. More than half the lockers had been thrown to the floor, and the others had their doors ripped off. Jack remained silent for a long moment. Another set of sneezes came and went. Frustrated, confused, and concerned, he tried to think of what to do next. In the distance, he could hear that it was windy outside, and in that wind he heard a sort of banging sound, as if things were being tossed around.

"No power but emergency lights. Dust and everything has been trashed. It's like everyone abandoned this place a while ago. Where is everyone?"

Alone, tired, and disoriented, Jack decided he would forgo changing out of the wetsuit, not that he had anything else to put on. He would be happy to walk the halls of the Massachusetts Institute of Technology in his dried, black wetsuit if he could find and talk to anyone. He moved to the main door separating him from the connecting public hallway. For a moment, he panicked that he did not have Barry's or any personnel's magnetic key to get in and out of the secure laboratory area.

As he approached the set of heavy double doors, it was clear he would not need one. Both doors were off their hinges and lying on the floor, heavily dented as if they had been battered down. Looking beyond them, Jack saw nothing but darkness, with the exception of small pools of emergency lighting. He saw debris and trash all around. Additionally, he heard the scurrying of small and not-so-small creatures. The sound of the wind and periodic banging was still in the distance but getting closer. With little hesitation, Jack proceeded to find a large metal rod for a weapon and began his trek down the dark hall. Although he was concerned there might be creatures with fangs and claws waiting in the night, dodging the litter and scattered mess filling the once pristine hallway was a danger as well. It took longer than he wanted, but he finally made it to the Charles River exit of the MIT School of Engineering. As he emerged, he was struck by how cold he suddenly was. The wind was coming from the east, over the river. Instead of the expected crisp fall wind, the breeze delivered a foul smell, a combination of sulfur, garbage and feces. The banging sounds he had heard inside came from various signs, rusted and broken barrels, trash cans, and posts that were off their mounts or not tied down. Also eerily evident was the absence of all traffic and nearly all sounds.

"What the hell…" Outside now, he was doing his best to take everything in.

Jack gripped the metal rod and looked in all directions to make sure he was not in danger. Still shocked by the lack of city sounds, it took him a minute to realize that he could make out darkened images of familiar buildings that stood like silent sentinels, void of all light and life, watching over a dead city. He expected to see Cambridge and Boston alive with Halloween revelers and streets filled with bright lights and festive crowds. Instead, he looked around and saw nothing but debris, ruin, and emptiness in the darkness. Only the stars' illumination gave any indication that he was truly in the once bustling city. Jack took his time and walked up the deserted Massachusetts Avenue toward the river. No cars, no people, no dogs—nothing was on the road. As he walked down the middle of the street, he turned many times to see if there were any signs of life, either on the street or in the tall buildings around him. He set his gaze on the two largest buildings in Boston and a series of other smaller structures, but they too were completely dark. The closer he walked towards the east, the more the foul smell grew with each gust of wind.

"Where is everyone? What happened?" he asked.

He had never seen Cambridge, or any metropolitan center, look as if it had been suddenly evacuated of all living things, leaving nothing but debris, wreckage and trash. The closest he had ever experienced such emptiness in the city would be in the very early mornings when he lived in Boston. But people were just asleep and things were in order. It was just lonely then but now, this place was desolate, devoid of life, light and noise.

The periodic howls of distant animals, the rattles of broken street signs and lamps, and the vile wind were the only things that answered him. He continued walking in his now-dry wetsuit until he came to the banks of the Charles River. With no sign of human life or movement anywhere, he was glad to see that at least the river separating Cambridge and Boston was still running, maybe even filled with living creatures. As soon as he had that comforting thought of life, he saw the silhouettes of three dead bodies floating down the river under the dim glow of the starlight. It was not a fast river; it moved the bodies by him at a slow, even pace, which allowed him the chance to identify them as human but not make out their features. The smell was the strongest at the river.

"What..." he exhaled.

A thunderous boom caused him to jump several feet toward the river. The powerful, distant boom echoed from behind him but soon faded away. While still catching his breath and making sure his footing was on firm ground, he watched the horizon starting to glow. It was in the distance, and at first it looked as if the horizon itself was brightening, but then it became clear that an object was moving in his direction. He backed away until he was mere feet from the riverbank, but he kept his eyes on the approaching light. As the horizon's edges returned to their nighttime darkness, the light coalesced into one point that kept expanding in width the closer it got to him. It grew to a formidable size in just a few seconds, with an accompanying increase in brightness.

"What now? What's going on?"

As it approached, it lit up the dark and desolate streets to near-daylight conditions. The air around him seemed to become electrically charged as a massive rock, a meteorite, fully ablaze with a blazing tail of fire, moved over his city, him, the river, and beyond the Boston skyline, now as bright as the high-noon sun. The distinctly acrid smell of sulfur dominated all others and was accompanied by a roar louder than the most powerful jet engine he had ever heard. But the reverberations, the ground shaking in its wake, were the most frightening, indicating its power and force even as it traveled hundreds of feet above him. As the fiery mass began to grow smaller, Jack returned his attention to the river, hoping to see things more clearly in the last moments of its fading light. His eyes hadn't deceived him; both up and down the river, as far as he could see in each direction, clumps of bodies followed its current.

He immediately staggered back, heart racing and gasping for breath. His throat went dry, and his stomach felt as heavy as lead. Clear of the river now, he found he could not stand. Down on all fours, Jack was at a loss; he had no idea what to do.

"That was a meteor," he said. "Why are there dead bodies in the river? There must be hundreds of them!"

The light of the passing meteor had faded, along with the sound and the vibration below his feet; the city fell back into silent darkness. Oddly, though, the wind was no longer blowing, and the air felt warmer. The strong smell of sulfur and now metal hung in the air. Jack felt as if he had been on all fours for several minutes before he finally sat back on his legs and looked toward the Boston skyline. He was still trying to make sense of this strange yet painfully familiar place when he saw a bright reddish-orange light slowly growing on the horizon. At first he thought it was the sun rising, but its rapid expansion and the fact that it was night didn't make any sense.

"Something else? Another one," he said mournfully. "Another meteor?"

He was sure that the meteor's approach from the west was more white and red, though. This light seemed like a sun. As his mind whirred with possibilities, a blast of wind, like that from an explosion, knocked him flat on his back. He covered his eyes as the bright light grew larger and larger, as if the sun were landing on the planet. In a twist of good fortune, Jack was flat on his back when the wind began to stream by, carrying torrents of debris above him while the earth heaved and quaked beneath him, with no hint of subsiding. Finally, as the light transitioned from brilliant to blinding, Jack heard the blast front as the thunderous explosions multiplied. He clasped his hands over his closed eyes, but the blinding light pierced through, and heat exploded all around him. Searing pain spread throughout his body, as if he were melting. He would have cried out, but there was nothing but a heated vacuum with no air to consume.

*No...not again...*

# All Saints' Day: Fourth Life

## 1:15 a.m., November 1

Jack jumped to life in his chamber. He called out and barely heard his own voice. The heat, bright light, and deafening sound of destruction all around him as the earth shook below him had subsided.

In its place were silence and the warm iridescent blue water, giving him the false sensation of floating. Jack struggled to catch his breath, again. It took time, and his hands instinctively went to the sides of the tank.

"I'm…I'm back here…again…" he croaked out. His right hand found one of the emergency release buttons—it was like an instinct now—and again the hatch of his sensory deprivation tank opened. Jack pulled himself out, with some difficulty, and was greeted by the strong smell of chlorine in the air. Exhausted, he pulled himself up to a sitting position. He found the smell of chlorine overwhelming and did his best to get out of the tank and closer to the floor in the hope that the smell would dissipate. He continued to cough; his efforts to get up and out of the tank and to the floor were punishing, leaving him nearly breathless. Unable to stand, he dropped to his knees and kept close to the floor. The lab appeared to be in the condition he remembered it being in when he first came in, except that the lighting was slightly brighter and the smell of chlorine was potent. In the areas that were closest to the lights, he could see what seemed to be greenish smoke of varying thickness. At first Jack was sure it was smoke from a fire, but the distinct shades of green and the lack of fire confused him. Still, he decided to stay close to the ground in the hopes that there would be breathable air there, as there might be in a real fire.

Jack pulled his neoprene cap off and used it to cover his nose as he continued crawling on the floor. The cap seemed to be helping, but his eyes were really starting to itch, and his lungs tingled as if they were inflamed.

*Barry's a soldier and blows up everything, including me. And then a meteorite destroys everything and I'm killed again...what now?*

He focused on searching for the exit, but as he moved just beyond his tank he had a clear view of the two tanks behind his. First, he saw that the hatches were open. Then, right below them, he saw two people lying still at the foot of the closest tank. Struggling to catch his breath and any clear air, he moved closer to see if they were alive, with the greenish smoke ebbing and flowing around him. Once he was close enough, he realized who they had to be. As still as death, a young man with blond hair and pale skin sat upright, his arms around a pale-skinned female with red hair. They were nestled together in an embrace, eyes closed and with peaceful expressions, both in black neoprene wetsuits.

"Owen?" Jack whispered. He nudged the young man's foot in the hopes that maybe he was passed out. There was no response. As he got closer, he touched the woman's leg—he guessed it was Rory King—but she too did not stir with his touch, which was met with stiff resistance. Although he wasn't a medical doctor, he could tell by their stiffness and the smell of bowels that managed to pierce through the thick chlorine that they were dead; rigor mortis had taken hold of the bodies.

"They...must have been here for days," he said.

Even with his cap providing some protection from the smell, he was becoming lightheaded. He looked at the pair and felt sad that this was his first meeting with the two other subjects. And then he saw that both of them still had their own neoprene caps in their hands, as if they too had used them for a similar purpose. Jack shook off the image and moved as quickly as he could toward the exit, still crouched low to the floor, but his fatigue was becoming overwhelming. The poorly lit room seemed to become darker, as if the green smoke was getting denser, but he was not sure if it was his eyesight that was now failing or if the place was filling up with more gas. His eyes stung, and his lungs were starting to burn in earnest.

Finally, Jack found himself at the door that led to the control room. Instead of standing or kneeling to open the door, he tried to push it open from his current position. Much to his surprise, it opened with ease. Still nose and body to the ground, he moved as well as he could through the small control room.

Another body sat in a chair, slumped over the control panel. Jack thought he could make out technician Marco Sykes's outline, with his short brown hair and yellow sneakers.

"No," he heard himself quietly say.

The effort to say anything was exhausting. With another door in front of him, Jack was fighting the overwhelming desire to just sleep. Although he was sure death would take him, like the others, he found it too difficult to move. He eyes and lungs burned. His nostrils felt as if the inner skin was on fire, and his vision narrowed further with every passing second. A sense of both cold and numbness crawled up from his limbs and continued until it reached his torso and head. Jack tried again to move, but he felt too tired. Rather than continue to fight for life, he decided to just lie on the floor and wait. He was surprised that he no longer felt the floor beneath him. Even though he was still feeling numb, he was no longer feeling cold.

*What are you waiting for? Get...up...move...*

He became confused by his own question but then was distracted by his eyesight tunneling to a fine point. His muscles released their tension, finally, after fighting too hard, and he felt as if he was just on the verge of falling asleep. As he faded, he thought he saw a soft, growing light. It reached a certain point but then faded. Jack's face relaxed, eyes heavy, and he felt happy to be dozing off.

*Is this...death too? Am...I...dying?*

# All Saints' Day: Fifth Life

# 1:15 a.m., November 1

Jack jumped with a start, like an old man catching himself from falling asleep at the wheel. Waking this time was far less dramatic than the last couple of times, but he was still feeling awash with anxiety, fear, and fatigue. Rather than finding and pushing one of the escape buttons, he took a moment to orient himself and just wait and think. It was silent, and with the sole exception of the luminescent blue-tinged saltwater, there was no other external stimulus. After what seemed to him to be several minutes, he found that his breathing was stable, and he was finally calm. He was about to push the button again but hesitated.

"No, no, no, no...Every time I open the hatch this dream or insanity starts."

It was hard to resist the urge to just get out of the tank, but he waited, doing his best to ground himself in what he hoped was reality and not some crazy dream or hallucination.

"But all those places, they were so real," he said to himself.

He focused on keeping his breathing level and watched the water swirl and ripple with every slight move he made.

Unexpectedly, the tank's hatch opened slowly, and the familiar face of his long-time friend peered in.

"Hey, Jack? You all right?" Barry Parker asked.

After all the dreams, visions, or hallucinations he had experienced, Jack did not expect a low-key, matter-of-fact question to follow an ordinary opening of his chamber. He felt as if he were going to choke up and lost his voice. Embarrassed to be so emotional, he cleared his throat and pulled himself up. His friend helped him, continuing to talk as if nothing unusual had happened.

*Am I going crazy? But it was so real.*

"Looks like you had some massive dreaming going on there. Jennifer and Marco wanted to spring you an hour ago, but you settled down. I think you fell into theta-REM and didn't look back."

Still silent and finding himself disoriented and tired, Jack was relieved to see that the laboratory was the same as he remembered it from what seemed like many lives ago. He made no effort to hide his fatigue and put his full weight on his friend, both to help him move and to feel that he was real. The dark, mildew-ridden small room still housed the three sensory deprivation tanks, and it was easy to see that he was the last one to emerge. He remembered Parker telling him that the other subjects—Owen, the computer kid, and the blind therapist Rory—had started earlier.

"There was a surge of electricity a couple of hours ago that knocked out our sensors, but there seemed to be no distress," Barry said. By now, Jack was able to stand unassisted. He had his neoprene cap off and felt his strength returning rapidly.

"Welcome back," Dr. Jennifer Green said. Her voice was pleasant even over the PA system, and her smiling face from behind the control room's Plexiglas was reassuring. To her immediate left was technician Marco Sykes, who looked up from the control panel and gave Jack a thumbs-up before looking back down at some disassembled pieces of equipment.

"It…It was crazy, Barry…I think I'll have to take a break from this for a while," Jack said. His throat felt dry, and it still stung from the distinct taste and smell of chlorine. Barry guided him to the chamber's preparation and dressing room, and it was clear to see that his worry had disappeared and that his friend was now off to the next thing. Jack nodded that it was okay to let him go. Now having the strength to stand and move without assistance, Jack was able to look around to make sure he was not in another altered state or dream. Everything appeared to be normal.

Jack gave his friend another nod and watched him smile and start to walk back to the control room, already engrossed in his tablet. Suddenly, he noticed that Parker was in his typical food-stained, off-white lab coat, with faded denim pants and a gray rugby shirt underneath. Jack blinked his eyes to make sure he was not dreaming.

*Costume party tonight?*

The image of his friend stuffed into a Batman costume was a dim memory. Nonetheless, Jack was positive that before all of his wild visions, his friend was in costume, getting ready to leave for a party with his girlfriend, Jennifer.

"Hey, Barry," Jack started. "Did you go to the party with Jennifer and come back or something?"

His friend turned and chuckled.

"Yeah, right. Like I got time. And don't bring up anything about parties," his friend added. He motioned with his head to the control room he was entering.

"Marco and Jennifer were pissed when I called them in for tonight's session. They like you and everything, but they were really looking forward to being Dorothy and Scarecrow tonight." Without much thought, his friend disappeared into the control room, leaving Jack confused. He remained standing with support of the doorjamb. A full minute went by before he fully processed what his friend had said. Until then, everything had seemed as if he were out of the tank and back to his real life.

"But I can't be wrong," he said.

Jack proceeded to the dressing area. Again, everything looked the same, and he found his clothes and belongings right where he had left them earlier, or at least the way he had thought he remembered them. It felt like he had been away for hours, hours filled with craziness and shocking events, and it took him a while to realize that his belongings were right where he thought he had left them. All was in place and just the way he remembered it—until he picked up his wristwatch. It was still a large gold watch, but rather than having the white face and Roman numerals, it had a black face with Arabic numbers.

Jack felt his knees get weak, and he took a seat. He sat motionless, looking at the watch, for a long time.

*The watch is different. And Barry wasn't dressed in his costume. Jennifer and Marco were going to go to a party? Everything's the same but these small differences...How? Why?*

It was hard to think about, let alone understand, what was going on.

*Another dream? Visions? But why so subtle?*

Jack had a strong urge to see what was the same and different outside and beyond the laboratory. He felt a sudden flood of anxiety. He dressed as quickly as he could and got everything together. Normally he would have said good-bye to his friends and colleagues, but he just wanted to get outside and home to see if anything else had changed.

After five minutes of confusion as to where he had parked his car, he found the vehicle's parking space and the environs all as he remembered. It took only thirty minutes to get to his hometown's expressway exit because there was no traffic on the highway at 2:00 a.m. Seeing every light, street, and traffic sign in place, he felt himself relax. Still, the road did seem emptier for a night that was supposed to be filled with revelers.

*No way everyone finished at two and left for home.*

Once he was off the highway and driving through his

town, he expected the homes to be dark with people sound asleep, but many streets were devoid of public street lamps, and there were no driveway or tree illuminations, and only an infrequent light could be found.

As he turned down his street and approached his own home, he immediately noticed that all of his lights were on, and that someone was sitting on his porch. This was in sharp contrast to the rest of the neighborhood. His ease and comfort evaporated; he was once again vigilant. It took some effort to see through the darkness that the person on the porch was feminine, and it looked as if she had a dog on a very long leash.

"Now what the hell is this about?"

As he pulled his car in behind another one he had never seen before, most likely belonging to the woman still sitting on his steps, his calm shifted to irritation and anger. He moved quickly from his parked car and walked with authority toward the waiting woman. He was absolutely sure he did not park at the wrong address, and all the defining telltale signs that it was his home—the number, color of the house, and all the structural nuances—confirmed there was an intruder on his property. In addition to the intruder and nearly all of his home's lights burning bright, another thing stood out: strong smells of cooked meat, garlic, and other wonderful odors hung in the air.

Once he was within about eight feet of the steps, he finally noticed that the dog was patiently sitting, with its tail wagging furiously. The beagle ran toward him and jumped to meet him as if she had not seen him for years. He gently patted and rubbed Clover's ears. His instinctual smile disappeared, suddenly replaced with surprise and confusion. The younger woman with red hair and pale skin stood up to meet him. The way she looked at him seemed odd, and it immediately indicated that she might be visually impaired. She was well dressed in tan slacks and a matching blazer over a crisp white blouse, topped with a fashionable brown coat; she gave the impression of a professional woman home from work sitting with her dog. His inner mind flashed to the dead couple he saw earlier in a gas-filled room at the foot of a sensory deprivation tank.

*Is this possible? No. Is any of this shit possible?*

Jack simply stared at her for a moment longer before he had enough moisture in his mouth to say her name.

"Rory King?"

"That's right. It's great to meet you, finally," she said. Her voice was even, calm, and oddly inviting. It was not sensual but embracing.

"You may or may not know this, Jack, but I am blind and cannot see you," she said as she extended her right hand to shake his. He willed himself out of his trance as images of her death materialized right in front of her.

"Yes," was all he said.

The uncomfortable silence and the stillness of the cold night created a strange juxtaposition with the wonderful cooking smells emanating from his house.

"Well, let's get right to it," Rory said.

Jack said nothing. He was tired suddenly. His excitement that he made it through his crazy dreams vanished. He knew that whatever she was going to say would not be reassuring.

"You might have experienced some strange events. Almost like living different lives," she started.

"Yes," Jack said. Both relief and fear gripped him. She had just acknowledged what he had experienced, but if that was true, it meant his visions were all real.

"It is true. And although I'm not a scientist, I've had at least twelve lives to figure this out. A couple of lives were very brief, but—"

"Did you die in the lab from some kind of greenish mist? Smelled like chlorine and burned your eyes and nostrils?" Jack interrupted.

Rory King nodded her head and smiled.

"Yup. Didn't get much of a learning experience in that short life," she commented.

"That's all I've had. They've all been short lives," Jack said.

Rory's head tilted as if she were interested in hearing what he had to say. He spoke in a lowered voice as he recounted just how brief but horribly long his experiences had been—different worlds that were just like his but different in important ways. As he collected his thoughts, his legs felt somehow rooted to the ground, but he was able to move them with ease. It was an odd sensation that he pushed out, focusing instead on his words.

"I was in a place where my best friend was a commanding officer of some military installation. He told me that they were trying some kind of time-traveling thing, but it ended up being some kind of parallel universe," he said.

"Yes. Owen and I found out that you arrived three days after we showed up. You didn't make it," Rory said quietly.

"Yeah...He blew up the installation...But why?"

Rory's response was immediate.

"Because they created three holes or conduits that allow travel from one multi-universe to the other. If the Russians in that universe were able to figure out what we did, there would be more holes. More of us," the woman explained.

Jack felt his dog jump on him again. As he listened, he felt his legs getting very tired, and the odd sensation was less noticeable. He dropped to one knee and started rubbing his dog's head. He sensed that his pet knew he was distressed.

"In one universe, we came to a world divided in a war between NATO and Russia. Owen and I lived there for three years, but like over three million other Americans, we died in some kind of nuclear explosion. In another world, we escaped to a fallout shelter high in the Appalachian Mountains to avoid the direct hit of a twelve-mile-wide meteor that was supposed to hit somewhere in the Northern Atlantic. It didn't matter, though. The blast front destroyed everything around us, and we suffocated in a blast-proof bunker. And then there was this one time when we opened our tanks to a lab filled with deadly chlorine. We decided just to sit it out and move on to the next world."

"How did you know there was going to be a next world? Are they all short? Do we always have to die right after we've arrived?" Jack asked.

"Before those places, I lived two separate lives on two different Earths. One Earth was a planet filled with two kinds of humans, one just like us and another hominid you and I know as the Neanderthal. In that history, that prehistoric species prospered right beside ours. The result was a great deal of interbreeding, with great music, literature, and architecture. There were also no wars. It was amazing," she said. In her description, he felt her sadness, as if she truly missed that world.

"You miss that place?" he asked. *Neanderthals...But they are extinct...*

"Sure do," she said immediately. "It was wonderful. It was a place I wish I could go back to. There had never been world wars or massive open conflict, and they had focused instead on medical health. The advances in health sciences were amazing." She fell silent, and it was easy to see that she was sad. She took a moment to move on to the next subject.

"It was a great world where I lived for well over a century. The other universe had an Earth where the United States had invaded all of Canada and Central and South America to form the United State of Americas sometime after the Civil War. By 1905, the entire western hemisphere was under complete control of the federal government located in Philadelphia. Every citizen—male or female, black or white, ages fifteen to forty—they were all required to serve in the armed forces, either directly or indirectly, to aid the 'Great Expansion.'"

"My God," he said. Even as she continued, Jack found himself running through the massive differences in history based on a series of actions that were never taken in his world. *That could have happened...Union decides to keep expanding south and north...And with no restriction on supply of soldiers? Men and women? It's like World War II...*

Rory continued as if she expected that very response.

"As a result, those United States took on a policy of isolation, leaving the European countries to fall into disarray and eventual economic and social chaos after the First World War. I lived about forty-five years in that world among xenophobic, chauvinistic, and paranoid people who watched the world around them die from behind their walls. After a while, I was glad to leave that world."

*No America to balance out the world. That could happen.*

As she spoke, Jack had been listening intently while he rubbed his dog's ears and head. When she paused, he noticed that his dog's collar was a dark color, blue or black, but it definitely was not red. This difference brought his attention to a bone-shaped dog tag inscribed with a different name. Instead of Clover, this dog was named Penny.

"How did it end?"

"That world?" Rory said. "I don't know. I died of cancer when I was seventy-seven years old. Owen told me that China was a growing democracy and linked up with India. He died before hostilities between the West and the Far East broke out."

Jack took a deep sigh and finally stood up. He was tired and anxious about what was happening to him. There was another odor of food wafting out of the kitchen vent out back. The succulent smells were carried by the cool November air. Jack did have a question that was rooted in the here and now.

"By the way, is Owen the young man with blond hair in my kitchen? Any reason why he's obviously cooking up a storm at two in the morning?"

Rory smirked and waved him over to come up the stairs to his own house. She reached back and used the railing to guide herself up. His dog joined her quickly. She spoke as she took the five stairs deliberately and carefully.

"Before we made it here, we were on a world that was

near desolation. Photosynthesis was profoundly hindered as a result of Earth's spin slowing to a stop. By the time we arrived, the food chain was knocked out at the bottom, and everything else followed. There were mere islands of civilizations left. Little rain, a full year of night followed by a full year of life and death, and weakening of the magnetic field led to disaster. Best guess was that there might have been a few million people left at the end of the thirty years after the catastrophic changes in the Earth got started. We left as soon as we could."

Jack stopped at the door of his own house. As he opened the door, he turned to face Rory.

"You can leave? How?"

He felt his heart begin to race and a sudden surge of excitement and hope must have been audible.

"Owen and I jumped off of a crumbling skyscraper after two years of suffering," Rory said without emotion.

"Oh," was all Jack could muster up. *Holy crap...*

"Yeah."

"You and Owen? You killed yourselves?" Jack asked. *How could you just do that?*

Rory answered his unasked question.

"Two years of no food, no moderate temperature, raiders fighting and killing others for food, water, or worse...Trust me. That world, that place...When Owen suggested we simply end our lives, I jumped at the chance...no pun intended."

Jack gave a nervous chuckle but was deep in thought about how they could just kill themselves—even if they thought they might come back. His heart and stomach sank as she continued inside. He immediately noticed that his home's foyer was nearly empty, except for one table and an area rug. Rory dropped down to release Penny from the leash and then handed it to Jack while she continued.

"When we arrived here three days ago, Owen went on a food spree. We'd been to many worlds before, but that last one had an effect on him," she said.

From his kitchen doorway, Jack saw a young blond man

moving from stove to refrigerator to table in swift motions. In midstride, he looked over at Jack and smiled.

"Hi! I'm Owen Mason. Rory telling you everything?" His voice was young and strong. What was interesting was that the young man stayed focused on his moving and cooking, and didn't really wait for an answer. His relatively round body and boyish look caught Jack by surprise. In death, he looked older. Now, he looked youthful, which made sense because he was in his early twenties. Rory was unfazed by his distraction and responded as if this had happened a lot.

"I got this, Owen. I take it you'll have dinner or breakfast or whatever soon?"

"About an hour. Lamb, beans, steak, potatoes, beer, wine for you, and this place has shrimp," he said with zeal.

"After that last place, I'm all in."

"Hell yeah," he said.

Jack did not know what to say. Two strangers giving him a fantastic story about multiple Earths and parallel universes, and he was just rolling with it? Crazy!

"I had that much food here?" Jack couldn't imagine that he did, in any universe.

"No. We had a chance to gorge ourselves earlier but we stopped at a store before coming here hours ago and started after you left for the lab. Hope you don't mind," Rory said. It did sound like an apology.

*If I hadn't experienced what I had, I'd have already called the police.*

"We'll wait in the other room," she continued. She moved in front of Jack and headed to his front room, which was an office. As he moved behind her, he saw that in addition to the foyer and the dining room being devoid of furniture, save one table in front and a four-person dining table set, his once-cluttered office was joining the ranks of Spartan in its appearance. His computers and monitors were still on his desk, and there was one desk chair and a dining room chair from the other room. With two bones for his beagle to gnaw on, the empty room was just the way he had wanted it back when he started.

"So what this all means, based on our research, is that the theories about multiple universes that all the physicists thought might be true are, in fact, true. We are examples of that. We are not immortal because we do die, but we seem to almost reset at the exact launch point, yet in a different place in a corresponding universe."

There was silence. Jack was not sure what to say.

"Are you a scientist?" he finally asked.

"No. I'm a therapist by training, at least originally. But in a couple of the places we were at, we had access to very smart people, and this is as close as we could understand it," she answered.

Jack was still at a loss for words. He looked at his watch and could easily see the differences.

"I know this is all pretty incredible. If I hadn't had Owen with me I would have thought I was going crazy," she added. It was easy to see that she was being kind.

Jack suddenly wondered whether with all the small changes, were there also some big ones? Maybe his wife and son were alive. He looked around again and quickly realized that he wouldn't be Spartan, organized, and remarkably clean. This was what he did when he was anxious and sad. He never would have lived like this if they were both alive.

"So are there any big things about this world that are really strange?"

At first, Jack was surprised at how slow Rory's response was, especially in light of how open she had been. He watched as she seemed to find the right words to answer the question. A faint red light flashed silently on an old-style desk phone he had overlooked before. He pulled his gaze from the flashing light to his silent guest.

"Rory? Is there something really different in this world?" he asked again.

She nodded and then spoke in a low voice.

"It seems that ten years ago, there was a massive pandemic. It was smallpox."

"What? Wait...what?"

"I know, Jack. It was gone where we came from, but ten years ago here, in this world, there was an outbreak that killed one hundred and fifty million in North America," Rory said quietly.

Jack sat with that massive number. He was trying to remember how many Americans there were. Rory answered as if she had read his mind.

"There were about three hundred and twenty million when we left. Here, there's only half that. And it's the same everywhere. Russia, United Kingdom, China. Everywhere."

"That's just unbelievable."

"I don't know if you noticed, but there are only three people on this street. All the homes have long since been boarded up."

"So what's happening now?" Jack asked. He was just exhausted from the information.

*It's just too much.*

"The U.S. government is more of a military state, with all citizens involved in the armed forces in some role...active frontline defensive perimeters, lines of communications and supplies, medical services, intelligence, and weapons development. It's all a war machine industry. There really are no free markets, and the wage economy is narrowed to basic needs. We have taken a policy of isolationism, and although we seem to have great liberties, like extended leave and any port of call, we are expected...rather, I am expected, to produce four to five children with different donors. Not a totally bad thing if you're up for that," she said. There was a humorous tone to an otherwise horrible story.

The flashing light on the telephone continued to blink throughout their discussion. Annoyed and needing something to distract him, he picked up the phone. It was heavier than he expected, solid, and ergonomically pleasing compared to his smartphone.

"And this place has a thing with landlines for residential and office phones, facsimiles, and videophones. Don't ask me why," Rory added.

"*You have one message. Here is your one message,*" the recorded voice said. It took Jack mere seconds to identify the voice as his friend, Barry Parker, but it was the worry and anxiety contained in his voice that made him listen intently.

"*Ah, hey, Jack. The team and I just took a look at your preliminary brain scans, and they're looking a bit weird. The acetylcholine and a bunch of other neurotransmitters throughout your limbic system look as if there has been a massive buildup of activities. This part of the brain is where memories are stored, and it looks like you got a shitload of memories up there. I thought it had to be a glitch, but the other two subjects have the same thing, and theirs is worse. So when you get a chance, call me and we'll send a car up to get you in the morning or something. I want to talk to you before Colonel Walsh hears about this. Talk to you soon, man.*"

More telephone prompting came on, but Jack hung up. It made a very satisfying clunk in its cradle, something he had missed with his smartphone.

"So? What was that about?" Rory asked.

"It was Barry. He said that my brain looked as if I had a lot of memories going on."

"Almost as if you had lived another life," Rory added.

"As if," Jack said.

Jack looked around for his dog and realized that she and her bone were gone. The smells of so many meats and blends of spices were now at their peak. As if to break his dark thoughts, he heard a young man in the other room call out.

"Okay, you two. Forget about life for a while—grab a seat and let's eat! God knows what's ahead of us here in this place," Owen said.

Jack couldn't help but smile a little at the young man's enthusiasm.

"He does have a point, Jack. I've watched him eat

everything for the last three days, with little chance of slowing down," she said. Rory stood up and extended her hand to Jack.

"I'm familiar with this room and the others that got me here. Where we'll be sitting is all Owen's domain. Could you give me a hand?"

Jack felt suddenly embarrassed at not offering her assistance.

"Of course," he said.

He took her hand and curled it under his arm, just as he did when his wife was alive. It was a long-missed feeling that felt comfortable to him even though she was a stranger.

"Don't worry, Jack. We'll figure it out. We're all in this together," she said.

Whether it was her therapeutic voice, her warm hand grabbing his arm, or her smile that made him feel relief, he was not sure. The fact that she was comfortable with him and the young man spoke volumes.

"We may be spending a lot of time with one another," she added.

"Yes," was all Jack could add. As soon as he turned the corner, he could see that his beagle was sitting in the middle of the dining room, salivating at the feast, while Owen filled glasses with water. The entire table was filled with all kinds of food varying in colors, sizes, textures, and smells.

"Well, I guess we won't starve tonight," Jack said. He found his smile expanding at the look of glee on Owen's youthful face.

"We sure won't," Rory said.

# Twelve Years, One Hundred and Four Days: Twenty-Second Life

## 2:30 p.m., March 15

"And what did your son say, Captain Jack?" the young woman asked. She might have been fifteen, and the others, eight in total, varying in age by a year or so, mere boys and girls, waited with bated breath for him to finish his story.

The open fire, smell of deer cooking in the pit, with dogs of all sorts waiting patiently for their share of food—a perfect picture for a campfire trip in the woods. Sadly, they were in the middle of Boston, with barricades of ancient, rusted vehicles surrounding them. Groups of ten to twelve soldiers, all under the age of seventeen, well spaced and well armed with swords, knives, bows and arrows, and firearms of all kinds, filled the central area. What was once an old Boston armory built in 1741 to house the First Corps of Cadets prior to the Revolutionary War, and later established as tourist landmark, was once again an armory. Known as "the Castle," it was now the last holdout of young survivors of a massive pandemic that turned every person over twenty years old into violent, insane killers who walked the entire landscape as far as the eyes could see. The once urban northeastern setting was now desolate of life except for this organized pocket of survivors. Now, empty, decaying buildings, well-placed obstacles, pits and blockades, and well-arranged fighting units of young people were all that was between them and the Castle. And although it was far safer in the ancient castle of stone, mortar, and reactivated spears and spikes, Jack and his small troop would be the last line of defense to keep the dangerous mobs at bay before it became a complete defensive war.

*Dying in a castle is no way to live.*

Still vague on the source and reason of the desolation, Jack asked for details and the survivors he found told him that everyone over twenty went raving mad and killed everything. The only groups not affected were children and teenagers. The event was called "the Scourge." Jack's plan was to find a safe place away from the urban settings, relocate there, restock and rebuild—see what could be done to save this world's survivors. It was a common theme in his multi-universe travels. But in this time and place, they never made it out of the city. There was no place to escape to. Worse, Jack was afraid that Rory and Owen might have met a terrible end. Although it had happened before, this life seemed different. He missed them more and really wished they were there.

And similar to the last series of lives, he kept feeling as if he were more rooted in each world. He felt as if he could draw energy from the sky, especially when it was storming with lightning. Even here, in the desolate place populated by children, he could feel a surreal energy connection to the very planet itself. Jack thought he was once again close to figuring out some reason for this when a young voice asked him a question.

"Your son, Captain? What happened?" another young man asked. His name was Bennett. Jack realized that he was in the middle of a story when he drifted off.

"Well now, remember, this was before the Scourge and

when everyone lived together, in homes and families. There was no madness," Jack clarified. He took an additional moment and looked down at the small rucksack he usually strapped on his back. Filled with C-4, it was his personal self-destruct mechanism in case he was about to succumb to the virus himself, should it ever strike him. Because he was already older and not indigenous to this universe, it was unlikely he would succumb to the disease, and he had gone well over a decade to date unaffected.

"It must have been beautiful," another young voice chimed in. The voice belonged to Mavis. Jack was reminded that these children had no idea what it was like before the end of days. They were all four and five when he arrived.

"It sure was. It was a time of peace, food, water, and time for leisure…anyway. I had just told my boy, who was five at the time, that I had to know, 'Do you want to join the *Federation of Animals and Plants* or what?' It took him forever to answer 'Yes,' and then I heard him sniffle and go upstairs," Jack said. As he spoke, he stood and basted the deer carcass with fat. He saw the dogs inch closer. After a few seconds, he nodded to a group of five young ones still listening to come get food. They all remained glued to his story, but they were now using their own knives and makeshift plates to cut into the meat. Jack gave them room to get their first meal of the day.

"Curious what the big deal was about joining a wildlife magazine subscription, I went to his room and found him packing up some clothes and a couple of toys in his backpack. I looked at him and I could see he wanted to cry but was soldiering through it."

With the five young people done with getting their food, he waved to the others to come get some as well. He motioned them to eat and didn't miss a beat. Hs audience, hungry and ready for battle, still hung on every word, which always surprised him.

"'What's wrong with you, honey?' I asked him. He took a

moment to speak while choking back his tears. 'I said I would *join* the *Federation of Animals and Plants*, and that's what I will do,' he said. He was straight-faced and pulled together all his belongings to leave home. He was planning to join this wildlife federation as if it were a real place away from home, and I just wanted him to tell me if he wanted the magazine or not," Jack explained.

A couple of hands lifted to smiling faces and chuckles. Even though they were children themselves, they could see the cuteness of a five-year-old mistaking joining a magazine subscription for joining a real cause away from home at such a young age. Jack had lived many lives, and with each passing one he lived, he felt more connected to people. He was less afraid to remember things once painful and embraced every bit of joy there was, no matter how small.

Jack had told that story a million times and probably hundreds of times to this very group. Although his story reflected an innocence of youth in a bygone time of safety and peace, his troops hung on to the story, regardless of how many times they had heard it.

"That was so cute," Mavis said. She looked back down and cut up her meat and took another bite. Another girl finished hers and was back to braiding Mavis hair.

"Yeah…he was cute. That was a long time ago. Many lives away," Jack said. His voice trailed off as he spoke, but a loud horn above them caught his attention. Jack looked up and saw a young woman dressed similarly as the rest pointing to the west as she shouted.

"Damn it. We can't even get a quiet meal going before they show up," Jack said to himself.

"I got a massive mob—maybe two hundred all heading this way! They're heading down Tremont Street. They ain't moving fast but they're moving! And it looks like they're a bit more organized. They got stuff."

"Eat up people!" Jack called out. "Those who can shoot, make every bullet and arrow count and stay behind the barriers. The rest of you all, follow me so we can meet them halfway. The more we kill out there, the less that get to our last stand! Make sure you give some food to the dogs too!"

As he shouted orders, the various groups of children broke out into well-practiced squads. Balancing their food, conducting weapons checks, and surveying fields of fire were all part and parcel of surviving in a very dangerous world. Jack handed his rifle to Mavis and positioned her behind a car. She took the rifle with expert handling and managed to eat a large piece of well-cooked meat. Another soldier handed Jack his own piece of food. He took a small bite of the food and handed it to Lucky, his adopted German shepherd. She gobbled it up and followed him over the barrier. Another young man, Robert, threw his small piece to the dog as well. By now, there were close to thirty young men and women heading to a yet-to-be-seen massive mob, which likely meant hundreds of dangerous, mindless walkers solely interested in killing them for food. Brandishing swords, knives, axes, and other handmade edged weapons, his group, though smaller, was well practiced and armed. Still, six years ago, this group of thirty advanced troops numbered over a hundred. He pushed that sadness down, refusing to dwell on it just like not seeing Rory and Owen in this life.

"Unbelievable. Twelve years in this…place and I still can't believe we are living in the zombie apocalypse. Crazy," he muttered.

"How old are you again, sir?" asked another young man. His name was Andrew; he was maybe twelve.

"Sixty-six," Jack replied.

The gruesome sight was before them now: a disheveled, disfigured, bloody, and mauled wall of moving flesh made up of what were once humans. Worse, they were once people just over twenty years old and beyond before a virus attacked everyone that age and older. Some were even children he once knew, but most of the time they weren't. He and the others would always get the youth nearing twenty out of the camp, give them weapons and what provisions they could spare and send them out north to the mountains. If they kept going, Jack and the others would never have to kill them. It was always horrible to send them off. Fortunately, no one ever left alone and, more importantly, Jack and his people never had to kill them.

Jack looked out at the mob and took it all in. There were many more than two hundred. He had seen this kind of mass march before, but this time something was very different. He moved ahead of his small group of defenders to the exterior ring of abandoned vehicles and barricades. As he approached, the walking dead raised their hands in unison and threw things at him and his charge.

"What the hell!"

A series of yells and screams came from front and behind. A hail of bricks, rocks, pipes, metal, and anything heavy fell on and all around him. Hit and banged up, he heard a series of shots from behind him ring out, including arrows whizzing all around him. A massive hot sting hit him in the back, and he immediately fell to his knees. More shots and arrows flew until he heard Bennett cry out for his team to stop.

Jack looked up to see that the walkers in front were all struck by either bullets or arrows, and many were down. He moved his hand to his back and felt blood. He felt cold and could not feel below his waist.

*Oh no...friendly fire. This is going to be hard on the kids...*

Before he fell over he pulled his rucksack in front of him and opened it as quickly as he could. Lucky was right beside him and growling at a group of walkers who were twenty feet away. Mavis and Bennett were right beside him as well.

"Captain, we got to move!" Bennett said. The fear and desperation in his young voice were unmistakable.

Now on his side on the ground, Jack made sure the C-4 wires were attached and the plunger switched on to red.

"It's too late for me, Bennett. I was hit in the spine; I'm sure of it. Get everyone back. I plan to go out with a bang,"

Jack said. There was no pain in his back, but he was getting very cold.

"Friendly fire…Damn it! How could this happen!" Mavis cried out. Her hot tears splashed his face and her small hands cupped his face.

"You're just kids, Mavis. You're experienced but you're not a trained tactical unit. Now get out and get way back. This blast could be a big one."

Jack watched Bennett jump up and shoot the closest walkers and then use his sword to kill two more. Jack took Mavis's hand from his face and put it on Lucky's collar.

"Mavis, Lucky won't leave me unless you take her now. Go. Where I'm going next I'll be happier and safe. Go now and tell more stories. And if two other adults, Rory and Owen, come looking for me, tell them I'll see them on the other side," Jack said.

Mavis began to cry in earnest and only moved when Bennett came and pulled her and Lucky away.

"Give them hell, sir!" a young voice cried out from behind.

Still on his side, Jack flipped the safety on the plunger, and it flashed green when he depressed it. As soon as he let the plunger go, the explosion would probably take out a twenty-foot area. A flash of his friend Barry came to mind at the thought of arming his dead-man's switch.

"Now that's ironic…"

Jack watched helplessly as hundreds of slow-moving feet gathered around him. He felt some pressure in his legs and torso as he was being lifted off the ground. Paralyzed, he felt nothing but more cold waves and lightheadedness. He felt his grip slipping, and after just a moment more, when he was sure he was surrounded by the walking dead, he let his grip go. Like other times before, other times when he died by explosion, there was always the light first, then heat, and then the beginning of an explosive sound.

*It's always the same.*

# All Saints' Day: Twenty-Third Life

## 1:15 a.m., November 1

Jack opened his eyes slowly to near darkness. The only thing he could see was the luminous blue saltwater he was floating in while encased in his sensory deprivation tank. Gone were the days of reacting violently when he died and returned to the same starting place over and over again. In twenty-two prior lives, he had been a soldier, insurgent, survivor, scientist, and, on far fewer occasions, an adoptive father and grandfather in a quiet existence surrounded by friends and loved ones. He loved those times. And during those times he had gotten closer to his co-travelers Rory King and Owen Mason.

*Hmm…I wonder when they will show up. I completely missed them last time…*

Jack moved his lips and tongue; they were always the most fatigued and dry. He moved again and could see the luminescent water moving around and felt his leg and arm muscles flex with great effort, as if he had been asleep for years. But for the first time that he could remember, he felt a sort of energy, electricity, that made him feel both alive and at peace at the same time. Usually he felt this outside when he was out of his tank. It was unusual for him to experience this connected energy to the Earth so soon.

*Maybe I'm getting wiser or something.*

He was about to sustain a one-person debate when the lid of his tank opened up. The room air that flooded his tank was cold, and the tank lab was bright, even though he could tell it was only relatively bright compared to his sensory deprivation tank. The face peering in was round and pale, with blond hair and a smile.

"Mr. Jack Conan Martin, I presume?" Owen Mason said.

Jack was genuinely surprised. Usually it was some kind of rotation between Barry, Jennifer, or Marco who would be helping him out or, worse, no one at all, usually because some kind of awful series of events or catastrophes had occurred. It took some effort for Jack to find his voice, but it came sooner than he thought it would. The surprise of seeing one of his co-travelers must have helped. *At least I won't be alone from the start.*

"It's…nice to see you…Where were you last time?"

Jack started to move, and Owen helped him up and out of his tank.

"We got caught up with a group of kids; they were all about nine or ten, and they all had an even larger group of younger kids. The world was in shit—all of the adults over twenty went crazy and were all zombie-like. By the time we got them to a safe place, we were already a week over our time. I guess we couldn't bring ourselves to abandon the kids," Owen explained.

"Oh…I can…understand that," was all Jack said. As Owen talked, however, Jack felt a strong wave of energy run through him again, as if he were both alert and calm at the same time. He felt fully aware of his environment, which he had never experienced before.

"We found your group of kids about two years after they said you died. They were all holed up in a castle in the middle of Boston. Your giving your life up for them rallied them to the point of frenzy, they told us," Owen said.

"Really?" he asked. Jack felt sad that he had left them alone.

*They were just kids...*

"Sure did. Apparently, their frontline forces shifted from defensive to offensive. Then the others in the castle continued the fight. By the time we got there years later, there were no hostiles in the entire city and expanding suburbs."

"Wow!"

"Yup...and Rory found a cure for the Scourge, by the way," Owen said.

Jack coughed more due to his dry mouth than surprise.

"Really? What was it? What was the Scourge all about?" he asked.

"Apparently, this world had a problem with its mosquitoes transmitting some kind of virus that created profound neurological issues in the fetus. The government created a genetically modified mosquito to mate with the female and produce dead offspring. Instead, it enhanced this Zika virus, and it infected developing fetuses and all adults. The best of intentions leading to hell—2.2 billion were immediately infected with the Scourge and 1.9 billion with Zika within the first two weeks. You saw where it all went to," Owen explained. His tone and face conveyed deep sadness.

Jack's thoughts immediately flashed back to the kids he left behind, which for him felt like minutes ago.

"And by the way, Captains Mavis, Bennett, and Robert wanted me to say thank you if we saw you in the next life. They seem like great kids. We moved all our kids to their camp and stayed there until we both died," Owen added.

Owen had again read his facial expressions and social customs and cues, which surprised Jack; his friend, someone who was supposed to be suffering from autism syndrome, was doing very well in reading him. Baffled by his friend's newfound ability, Jack focused on a memory that stuck to him: the time he found his group of children, frightened and scared but amazed to see an unaffected older person. It was as if they had been lost and were found by a parent. It was heartbreaking at the time but easy for him to understand why Owen and Rory didn't leave them.

"That's pretty empathic and expressive for someone on the autism scale," Jack said. His neoprene wetsuit had already shed the water away from him, which now pooled by his feet. He held onto his friend and the railing to get his bearings and get his legs working again.

"I think after twenty-eight lives I might be engaging parts of my brain that I had not had the time to engage in just one life. By the way, I think you're going to find this world really interesting," Owen said. Jack looked at him and saw him suppressing a smile.

*So that's it. More time to develop your brain.*

Jack's mind raced as flashes of brain structures, words, formulas, and organic science ran through his inner mind's eye that were completely unfamiliar, yet at the same time, he could understand everything. Confused at how he knew things he had never studied or even imagined, he remembered that Owen said this Earth was interesting.

"Is it a nice place?" Jack asked. He was now able to stand without support. He took his cap off and stretched his back and limbs to make sure they were all working fine.

"It is what I would call a more 'magical' place," Owen said.

Jack gave his youthful friend a quizzical look. It was relatively bright in the room, and his eyes had adjusted, so now he could see that his friend was dressed in a long blue tunic, black pants, and dark boots. The really odd thing was that Owen sported a midnight-blue cape that at first Jack had mistaken as a black raincoat.

"You really have to see it to believe it," Owen added. Not giving him a chance to ask any more questions, Owen guided Jack to the dressing room, where he found that everything was in order. In fact, the entire lab and layout of the building looked nearly identical to how he had seen it over the lifetimes, but it was empty, ancient, and abandoned. Jack reminded himself that he had seen the lab and building more often in disarray than ordered. Suddenly, Jack found himself thinking about the concept of entropy and the expansiveness of space. Forgetting where he was, he thought about how he had missed such an easy concept as multi-universe theory and how it had to be accurate by the sheer magnitude of space and the infinite probabilities that at some points there would have to be repeating universes and worlds that would deviate in certain events, with decisions being made in one universe while the opposite might be made in another. Again, words, theories, formulas, and data filled his brain, all unknown to him but understandable.

"You know, I think I finally figured out how this could all be happening," Jack said.

"The multi-universe theory," Owen said with a warm smile.

"Yeah," Jack responded.

In addition to having clarity in a number of thoughts, Jack had an overwhelming sense of well-being and a growing awareness that he somehow felt connected to the yet unseen world outside the laboratory's walls. Additionally, his limbs, especially his hands and arms, felt as if they were filled with energy coming from his brain through his heart and torso and out through his arms. His legs felt both light and rooted to the floor. Although these sensations had been a growing experience with every passing life, the feelings currently seemed to be at an all-time high and at the surface of his very existence.

*What is this all about?*

Jack turned to tell Owen these feelings but saw his own clothes stacked neatly on a clearly straightened and cleaned bench. The waiting outfit was very similar to what his friend was wearing, but it differed in color. His pants and boots were a flat black, and his tunic and cape were a very dark maroon.

"Are we in the 1400s or something? A cape? A tunic? Really?"

"Trust me, Jack," Owen said with yet another warm smile and a gentle hand on his shoulder. "This place is far more different than the clothes. You know the way out. Rory and I will meet you outside. There will be some people who look like soldiers, but you don't have to worry about them."

Without further explanation, Owen walked out. Jack watched him carefully and couldn't help but notice that not only did his friend appear far more warm and kind than he had ever been, but he walked a little taller than the last time they had met, which was about two lives ago.

It didn't take Jack long to change into his new clothes. He found that his typical grogginess was absent, and he kept having multiple thoughts about things he had always wondered about, like spontaneous combustion, psychokinetic energy, and electromagnetic fields and their energy being drawn and redistributed in a stream of plasma. How and why he had these thoughts and, more importantly, the answers, was a mystery in and of itself.

Jack didn't even notice that he was now dressed and walking out of the lab complex when he started to see groups of men and women of all ages, ethnicities, and in various states of health, all watching him. He smiled at them, and they smiled back. Some smiled in awe and wonder, and others smiled back out of nervousness and anxiety. As he walked, he sensed no fear or trepidation but rather unity and strength. The groups soon transitioned to columns of people, now holding torches, in the cold open air outside the complex. Jack looked all around and saw a skyline that was dark and deteriorated, as if abandoned. Although it was dark, it was easy to see that the buildings were not inhabited, but all were illuminated by a full moon. The moon, however, was far from its original sphere and instead in large floating segments, all near where a once intact moon may have been in his universe, but here it was shattered into five massive pieces and thousands of smaller parts.

"My God," Jack said.

His pace slowed, but he continued in the direction the

crowd led him. Finally, the span of people gave way to an expanse that stretched between where the Boston Public Library and Trinity Church still stood but was now all aglow with more torches and people about. The once tallest building of the city was a dark obelisk; most of its reflecting glass was gone at the bottom floors, but still many panes were intact above. And for the thousands of people gathered there, there was an eerie silence while the heat of the torches kept the air on that first day of November warm. Just ten feet away from him stood Owen, regal in his dark-cloaked garb. Next to him, staring ahead in the other direction, was a woman. Her feminine frame was indeed smaller than Owen's, but nonetheless royal and tall. She was dressed in a bright canary-yellow cloak with a hood that covered her entirely.

"'To himself everyone is an immortal. He may know that he is going to die, but he can never know that he is dead,'" the cloaked woman said in a deep though clearly recognizable voice. In the company of his two friends and the thousands of onlookers, Jack felt strong. It was a strength and power he had never fully experienced before. With every step he took to move closer, his mind became clearer.

"Samuel Butler," Jack said. "Fitting for us, I would say."

"I was thinking of a more French approach as 'To achieve great things we must live as though we were never going to die,'" Owen added. His smile was truly enjoyable.

"Marquis de Vauvenargues. He is not often quoted, but again quite apt for this meeting. Speaking of which, why are we here, and who are these people?" Jack asked.

*Shouldn't I be anxious or something?*

The canary-yellow-clad woman turned around to face him. She removed her hood to reveal the warm, kind features of his friend Rory. She seemed to look closely at him and drew near. Rather than hug him, both her hands embraced his face and held it as a mother would a child. Her eyes appeared as they always did, but she looked at him as if she were able to see into his entire soul.

"I can see you in spite of my blindness," she said.

"How do I look?"

"As I always imagined you would. A warm, kind, and gentle soul. Powerful and strong," Rory said.

Jack smiled and was about to say what he thought of her, but a reverberation ran under his feet, followed by another one—spaced out as if they were giant footsteps. At first it seemed far away, but it was clear it was getting closer. Rory's expression changed from warmth and kindness to determination and raw force. While the members of the crowd made a collective sigh and sounds of fear, they began to back away from the three of them. Jack looked down the street in the same direction Rory was staring. He followed her to where Owen stood; they were all transfixed on the same spot down the street. The footsteps shook the ground, and with every booming step closer, the crowd became more fearful. Jack was not only surprised that he had no fear, but he also had the conviction that he and his three friends could face anything that was coming.

"Dare I ask what is coming?" Jack asked. He was surprised that he was calm and able to just be curious about what was so large that it shook the street with every step.

"A dragon," Owen said.

"Kind of a dragon, minus the wings and half the size we think of. It does have the ability to direct fire, but it has no ability of flight, and unlike the ones we read about, these dragons cannot speak," Rory clarified.

"No conversation?"

"None. Shame really. I would have loved to have heard its voice," Owen said.

An elongated, loud roar echoed throughout the cityscape. Jack had an intellectual understanding of why the people were frightened and backed away from the approaching monster.

"And we are going to defeat it how?" Jack asked.

"Owen and I have powers that are unbelievable. Why? I have no idea. What's really strange is that the natives here showed us artwork, writings, books, and drawings about all three of us and the things we are supposed to do," Rory said.

"And do I have some superpowers?" Jack asked. Even as he asked, he felt his torso and arms electrify as if they were filled with current just waiting to be released. His other lives seemed as if they were echoes of a past symphony, shadows of his former self.

Before anyone could answer his question, a large *Tyrannosaurus rex*-like monster stepped into full view. Jack watched in amazement as it sniffed the air and looked around as if it had picked up a scent. Its massive head at the top of a thirty-foot body turned in their direction, and it was clear that the monster saw them. The massive creature moved surprisingly quickly toward them. The crowd broke and began to run, screaming. The creature was just upon them when Jack felt an energy surge and then watched it erupt from Owen's extended hands. In response, the giant creature crashed into an invisible wall. Stunned and shocked, the creature roared and charged again. Owen extended his hands again, and this time the monster was pushed back violently into a series of smaller buildings, crushing them in its fall. After the noise and dust settled, Jack watched the dazed and confused creature shake off the fall and get back on its feet. Rather than charge, the monster demonstrated its more dragon-like qualities, taking in a breath and blowing out a wall of fire. Again, the fire slammed into an invisible barrier, much to the monster's dismay.

Behind him, Jack heard the people gasp in shock. Their presence was somehow comforting. More energy drew up through the ground and up through Jack's chest and moved to his hands; he felt his legs rooted in the ground. Jack had an overwhelming urge to extend his hands toward the creature. It was a pressure, a need, a want that pressed him to do it. Feet firmly planted to the ground, Jack felt as if he were drawing energy from the very core of the planet and that the only release of the energy was to direct it out. He stood in a half-moon stance, extended his arms and hands, and watched beams of plasma and lightning surge from his fingers and burst into the monster's chest.

The creature fell backward and screamed in pain but did not stay down. It got up again, far more slowly this time. Not surprised or amazed at this unnatural power, Jack struck the creature again. He refrained from destroying it outright but was nonetheless amazed to see it struggle to get back up on its two massive legs. Jack was reluctant but was going to strike it again when he saw Rory floating several feet above and in front of him with her own hands and arms extended. Jack put his hands down and looked at Owen, who did the same.

"Well…that's something you don't see too often," Jack said to Owen.

Owen smiled and then chuckled.

"Oh, and fire, flames, and force fields are stuff we do all the time."

"Point made, Owen. You're quite right."

Jack looked back at his floating friend. Although her arms were outstretched, there were no obvious discharges of fire, flames, lightning, or plasma. In response, the monster looked angry at first and then confused. As Rory moved closer to the creature, it roared defensively and backed away. The closer Rory moved toward it, the faster it moved in the opposite direction. In less than a minute, the monster was gone, and in its wake was a trail of debris, dust, red-hot embers, and crumbled buildings. Massive roars of cheers and cries erupted from the growing crowd.

"What did you do, other than float?" Owen asked Rory.

"I told the dragon that it should leave and not return. If it did not, I projected an image of what would happen if it did not listen to me. I guess it decided that it wanted to live and left. Pretty smart, if you ask me," Rory said with a smile.

The cheering continued, and people came close but did not dare to get too close. Not quite sure of what to do next, Jack just wanted to talk to his co-travelers.

"So, anyone know why and how we have these powers?" Jack asked. His limbs felt tired, but then again, this was the only time he had ever drawn energy from the Earth's center and expelled it in the form of plasma and lightning through his hands. He guessed he should be tired.

"I have no idea, but before the dragon showed up, I was saying that there were images of three 'saints' who were to arrive on All Saints' Day, and I guess we are them," Rory said.

"Wow," Jack said. The crowds were chanting and now dancing in the streets, but it was easy to see that Owen looked worried. It was Rory who asked him what was wrong.

"Every place we go, there has always been some kind of struggle. If we have these powers, what struggle do you think will be here? If we could defeat a dragon, what more is there?"

"There are a lot of dangers on this Earth. And Mars and Venus have civilizations that are not too friendly," Rory said.

"How do you know that? More images?" Owen asked.

"Yes, and I can see into their heads, too. There is surprise but no malevolence. Still, your question is well put. What will the struggles be here?"

"Do we have to worry about these Martians and Venusians?" Owen asked.

"Not yet. They are watching us. Observing us for now," Rory explained.

Jack was going to say something, but Owen had wise words to share.

"'Watched keenly and closely by intelligences greater than man's and yet as mortal as his own; that as men busied themselves about their various concerns they were scrutinised and studied, perhaps almost as narrowly as a man with a microscope might scrutinise the transient creatures that swarm and multiply in a drop of water,'" Owen said, quoting H. G. Wells.

Even with the joyous yells and dancing, Owen's fitting quote was not lost on Jack or Rory. Her radiant smile made the distraction all worth it. But still, she returned to her original question.

"Struggles in the heavens are obvious. Here, I'm not sure."

Clarity of mind sprung up again, as if Jack's very thoughts were on fire. The answer seemed so simple, but Jack needed to make sure he was right.

"I think the challenge here is one of the greatest we have ever encountered," Jack said. He looked at Rory, who touched his mind as a feather would touch an arm.

"Power, absolute power...We must be careful that absolute power does not destroy us or the others absolutely. Wow. Never thought that would be a problem," Rory explained.

"Just when you thought this traveling was growing weary and tiresome, another venue opens, a more reflective one that is found in us rather than external to the world," Owen said thoughtfully.

Jack and Rory looked at each other in amazement. Owen, who was typically not known to be reflective or philosophical, or to pick up on social cues—until coming to this Earth—caught the meaning of the glance.

"I know, I know...I think after nearly thirty lives, the compiled life experiences have helped me utilize my social brain—pretty amazing if you ask me. Do you think we'll take these powers to the next life?"

"So far we've brought our knowledge and memories, and our brains have developed in response to each new place. I'm guessing yes," Rory said.

Jack watched the scores of men and women, elderly people, and children dancing in the streets, with music, food, and drink enhancing the festivities. The joy and happiness were unmistakable. It was clear as day that this world embraced the here and now, and Jack made a decision that he was sure was going to make all the future adventures on this Earth, and the next, fulfilling.

"Not only do I think we will have these powers, but more will come. But to make sure we keep our sense of who we are, the better angels of our humanity, I suggest we dance and have fun with the natives and have a great life here," Jack said. With that, he walked to a small group of children who were dancing in a circle and joined in. They were at first confused and unsure whether they were allowed to touch him, but with a little encouragement they drew him in. Similarly, Jack watched the same hesitancy followed by embracing as Rory engaged a large group of young women and men in an intricate dance; meanwhile, Owen launched into a wrestling match with some of the men. There was more laughter and dancing. For the longest time, Jack felt as if he were free. As if he were home. The next life was nothing but a distant curiosity, the way it was when he lived his first life. The difference this time was that he was happy.

*I hope we stay here for a while.*

# Neurogenesis

*Neurons that fire together, wire together.* - Donald Hebb

"Hey, Bobby? You're going to be late for work. Let's move," a strong, friendly female voice called out.

Robert Wright turned to look at the group home's van and smiled. He was happy that Gabby was driving him today. She had long, curly black hair and eyes and very dark skin with white teeth. Sometimes Darren, the home's director, or Michelle, the supervisor, would drive, but this time it was Gabby.

"Hi, Gabby! You look really nice today. Did you stay over?" he asked. He tried to zip up his heavy winter coat. It was difficult since it was smaller than he was, and even though it was sized extra large, he struggled to get it zipped up. He also had trouble tying his boots. It was hard for him to bend over without losing his breath. He did have his mittens in his coat pocket so he didn't have to look for them that morning. His coat was the color red he liked but it had small zippers for his big hands. He was still trying to zip up as she spoke.

"I sure did, boss. Peggy was sick and I took over for her last night," she said.

Still staring down, he focused all his attention on manipulating the small zipper pull onto the small teeth. His hands fumbled over the zipper and his stomach was pressing out of his maintenance uniform. He saw Gabby's hands reach out and take over for him. He let his hands flop to his side to allow her complete access. He smiled at her small, dark hands with red nails.

"Your hands are just too massive, my big boy," she said in her usual cheery voice.

"It's so easy for you."

"I have smaller hands," she said.

"I know. I like the color red," he said. He watched her carefully so as to make sure he could replicate her actions later. Darren always said it was a good thing to watch and learn. Her hands moved up and down quickly and, like magic, his coat was re-aligned and zipped all the way up to his neck. He looked down at his navy blue pants and smiled. He looked at Gabby and she smiled too. He stood still for a moment. He felt his face frown. He knew he forgot something. He had put something down on the ground so he could zip up his coat. Marsha and Debbie, the other two long-time residents of the group home for adults, had just brushed by him and boarded the van without a word.

"You're right, Bobby," Gabby said in her wonderful calm voice. "You forgot something, honey?"

"I know," he said. He continued to look down at his empty hands in the hopes that it would remind him of what he forgot.

"Hey, retard! How can you be so stupid?" Marsha hissed at him. He looked at her. She was very pretty and wore a lot of makeup but she was always mean.

"Hey, fat dumb-ass! You take the same brown bag with you every day! I don't have time for this," Debbie yelled from the back of the twelve-passenger van. She was not as pretty but she would sometimes walk naked into his room and try to kiss him. Debbie was smaller than him but she was scary.

"Now that is no way for young ladies to talk," Gabby said in a stern voice. He looked to see that she was talking to both Debbie and Marsha. It was then he remembered to look back. He saw his bag sitting right where he had left it when he first tried to zip his coat halfway from his group home and the bus stop. As he turned, he heard Marsha say, "Good job, retard!"

"That's enough, Marsha. We all forget things," Gabby said.

"Not every day like estupido," Debbie chimed in.

"I am not retarded or estupido. I have intellectual developmental disorder. That's what Barbara told me. They don't call it 'mental retardation' anymore," Robert said defiantly as he lumbered off the van to get his brown bag. He moved as quickly as he could and opened it up to make sure nothing fell out of the ancient, brown paper shopping bag. He touched each item to make sure he counted nine things.

"Photo ID card, sandwich, drink, morning snack, afternoon snack, afternoon drink, book, and two shoes. Great," he said. When it came to his book, he turned it over to make sure it was not too dirty or creased. He could never pronounce the title right and it was hard for him to read anyway but it was a gift from one of the smart doctors he knew where he worked. He felt smart every time he showed it to people.

He knew he had everything. It was a great reminder that Darren taught him years ago about how to count each shoe rather than calling them a pair. He had a hard time understanding how two things could be one thing at the same time. He marched to the bus and stepped up the two small stairs. He smiled at Gabby who smiled back.

"Finally," Marsha said.

He watched her plug her headphones into her ears. He looked at the nearly empty van and saw that in addition to Debbie and Marsha, Sally was on board too. She didn't live in the residence but she took the van to work with him. He was happy to see her, too. She worked at "*Mit*" just like he did but she worked in the kitchen cleaning the tables while he was the janitor's assistant. She was always quiet and looked sad. She was pretty, too, but she never wore paint on her face and nails like Marsha and Debbie did. She also wore the same white uniform while he wore the same blue one. He was always happy to see her, though. She didn't talk much but she was always nice to him.

"Good morning, Sally. You look very nice today," he said.

He remained standing while he waited for her to respond. She always did.

"Good morning," she said quietly. She looked at him as she always did.

"Is this seat taken, Sally?" he asked.

He was hoping she would say no. There were times when she would sound tired or sad. There were other times when she would have a mark on her face as if she had fallen down or had burned the skin on her pale hands. Gabby and everyone was nice to her even though she didn't live at the group home with them. Still, he always asked if the seat was empty and she had said no every time she was on the van for the last year. He was hoping she would let him sit next to her. Every day she said yes, and he would sit beside her and smell her perfume. It was nice.

"No," she said.

"May I sit here?" he asked as politely as he did the first time a year ago.

"Jesus Christ, dumb-ass! You might want to let her sit alone so you don't squish her! We go through this every time 'estupido two' is on the bus. Just sit down, retard," Debbie yelled out from the back.

Bobby ignored her. Darren, Gabby and Michelle always told him to ignore mean people, especially the people that called him "retarded."

"You can sit here," Sally said in her quiet voice.

"Thank you," Bobby said politely. He was smiling from ear to ear. He carefully sat on his half of the couch seat which meant that half of his bottom was hanging off the seat. It was worth it. It took just a moment to smell her perfume. Just then, the van started to move out.

"All right, people, you know the drill," Gabby said in her

74

sing-song voice. "Marsha – you're out at the Boston Public Library today and Debbie, you'll be going to the Arsenal Mall."

"That sucks! I hate the library! How come Debbie gets to go to the mall?" Marsha complained.

Gabby didn't respond. She never did.

"And my two favorite people will be my first drop-off today. First stop – MIT," Gabby said.

"*Mit*," Bobby said to himself.

The van moved slowly and Bobby felt happy about being dropped off first. This way he and Sally wouldn't have to listen to Debbie and Marsha argue and they would be able to get to work sooner. Bobby loved work. There were so many young, smart people. Lots of messes but lots of rooms with lights. He felt important. He had a uniform and a photo ID.

"It is really cool," he said. He was surprised when Sally responded. She rarely did.

"Yes, it is."

***

Bobby stood, transfixed, in the third-floor laboratories of Massachusetts Institute of Technology's Mechanical Engineering, Robotics and Artificial Intelligence departments.

He really liked the doll room. He smiled at all of the nearly completed, moving dolls. There were two completed, full-sized plastic dolls with faces and eyes that looked so real Bobby just wanted to touch them. He knew he couldn't. He knew they were girls because of the bumps under their smocks. Their long hair looked real but Dr. Ralph Peterson told him they were just wigs. He felt his own hair that was thin and short, very different from the wigs the dolls wore. They reminded him of the mannequins he saw at stores when the group home would go to the mall. He loved those times. He would stay by Michelle or Gabby so he didn't get lost.

Bobby moved his hand away from his head and bent over

to pick up more trash bins. His uniform felt too tight and his armpits were already sweaty after only three hours of working the third floor. This was his last stop before he started the second floor at the Hugh Everett Department. It was really different and not as fun as the third floor. Bobby looked up to see the dolls still looking at him as he moved his trash and cleaning unit to other trash and recycling receptacles. He continued to smile as he watched the dolls' eyes follow every move he made. As he mechanically picked up each bin and emptied it into its correct bin, he watched the dolls closely as he moved out of their vision. He waited and then saw two of them bend to look beyond the barrier to see if he was still there. His smile grew and he clapped his hands.

"Cool! You looked around! Really cool," he said aloud.

With no one in the large laboratory/robotic repair shop, he went back with his small cleaning rags and cleaner to wash all the cleared tables.

"You girls are really getting smart," he said. He moved to the very first table and began his careful cleaning as he spoke.

"You girls are quiet like Sally. I bet you would like her. Gabby and Darren, too. They are very nice. Marsha can be nice sometimes. She's always kind of nice when she gets back from her boyfriend's house. She visits him a lot. Debbie is nice too, sometimes," he continued as he methodically cleaned each and every table, chair, book case and bin. He looked up to see that they were still watching. Even though they had exposed wires at the joints of their tan casing and emotionless faces, he liked talking to them. He liked that they listened.

He kept talking until he heard the back door unlock and a group of people talking.

"Talk to you later, girls," he said. He continued cleaning as the group of young, smart researchers and professors walked by. They never said anything to him and kept walking as if he were not there. All but one. Dr. Ralph Peterson was different. He was an older man with short black and gray hair. He was plump but nothing like himself. He was also dark like

Gabby but his color was browner than dark brown. Dr. Peterson was one of the very first people to say good morning to him eight years ago when he got his present job. He also gave him his favorite book, his only book, which he kept in his work bag.

"Mr. Robert Wright," Dr. Peterson said. He was still walking just behind the group of young, smart people. He always called him by his full name. Bobby always felt like he was smart when he did. Important.

"Yes, Dr. Peterson?" Bobby responded promptly.

"You still reading my favorite book?"

"Sure am, Dr. Peterson. You think they will ever find medicine like they did for that guy in the book? Gabby says they will for me some day. Peggy, too, but when she reads the last pages to me, she insists on me guessing the ending." Robert said.

"And are you right, Mr. Wright?"

"Yup! I guess he stays smart, becomes president and helps people at residential programs," Robert said. He felt proud and patted the outline of the book in his oversized pants pocket.

Robert could not really understand Dr. Peterson's expression but then it changed to being happy again.

"Are my robots keeping you company? Any of them say anything?"

"No, Doctor. Can they talk? Will you ever be able to get them to talk?" Bobby asked. He was happy that he asked a question that made Dr. Peterson stop and come back to him. Bobby looked at him closely. Dr. Peterson seemed different.

"Talk? Someday. I would love for them to speak. Maybe even carry on a conversation," he said.

"That is hard to do, Dr. Peterson. A conversation is really hard. It's hard for me every day," Bobby said.

He was going to tell Dr. Peterson about Sally but remembered one of Darren's guidelines about sharing too much.

"A conversation, the ability to read expressions...hell, to even have expressions would be monumental. Right now they can only track movement and have mastered the ability to walk. Something that took us hominids thousands of years they can now do. But conversation and thinking? Pretty far off," Dr. Peterson said.

Bobby found himself really puzzled.

"But, Dr. Peterson? You and all these people are wicked smart. You can teach them to think! Gabby and Darren help me with everything!"

Bobby watched the older man look at him. He looked serious at first but then a warm smile emerged from the doctor's face. Bobby was relieved he didn't say anything wrong.

"Oh, Mr. Wright, we got our best people here working around the clock to generate sapient artificial intelligence. Not just here but around the world. We even posted our most recent logarithms and data on our website with the hope a team out there will put together the data in a way that will make our girls here live...with just the right configuration of algorithms, a cascade of neural activity could launch an entire thought. And thoughts beget more thoughts," the doctor explained while he pointed to the robots.

Bobby looked at him as if he understood. He really had no idea what Dr. Peterson was saying. Suddenly, Bobby remembered to ask his long-standing question.

"Oh, Dr. Peterson, I have to get into the think room to empty the garbage and recycling. The last time I was here, no one answered the door and I don't have a code to get in."

Dr. Peterson turned to look at him for just a moment. Finally, he smiled.

"Oh? You mean the 'think tank'? Yeah, we've been pretty busy in there. Lots of math and stuff," he said with a twinkle in his eye. "Come with me, Mr. Wright. I'll let you in."

Bobby put his disinfectant and cleaning rags on the table and retrieved two mid-sized barrels from his cleaning cart to bring with him. By the time he was right behind the doctor, Bobby saw him putting his code in. It always started with three point one four one five, and then went on for about a minute.

"That's a long code, Dr. Peterson," Bobby said. The code was by far the longest he had ever seen, or rather heard, as each push of the button made a chirping sound. He was positive he heard twenty-three chirps in total.

"It's long but it's easy for me to remember," Dr. Peterson said. The heavy door unlatched and he pushed it open. As Dr. Peterson stepped through, Bobby heard a cacophony of voices talking. It was the same group of smart people that were ahead of Dr. Peterson in addition to others that were working at various computer consoles, workstations, and tables. While the room was well lit, Bobby was always surprised to see that the walls that went around the room were entirely filled with symbols, equations and numbers he never knew what to make of. Before Dr. Peterson got too far, Bobby took a moment to ask him another long-standing question.

"Dr. Peterson? What are all those numbers? The numbers on the wall?"

Dr. Peterson turned to face Bobby. Even though his eyes were still sparkling, his smile grew.

"Those equations are the logarithms of life, an expansive formula of algorithms, numbers and theories that create artificial intelligence, or sapience. It is the code to teach the robots out there to learn, understand, innovate and make decisions. Every piece of data is put on the wall first, sifted and distilled and then inputted into the computer for later cranial distribution. Someday, maybe in twenty years, it will be ready," he said.

"And those numbers will make them smart?"

"Yup, but it will take a series of other numbers to connect them all to start the thinking. And once it starts, the thinking will never stop for them."

Bobby watched the doctor look around the room. There were three people at one section that had less on it that were adding to the insanely long formula. A sudden thought popped into Bobby's head. His mouth was speaking before he even knew it. Still, Bobby looked at the entire wall, at symbols and numbers that made no sense to him.

"Can those numbers make me smart?"

Bobby's eyes settled on the last empty section. As the three researchers added just a couple of computations, there was another person at a computer console that was speaking into a computer. Bobby suddenly smelled old food, garbage and smelly bodies. It was thick in the air. He wrinkled his nose and saw Dr. Peterson smiling at him.

"Those equations are to make the robots do what we take for granted. Anyway, my boy, we're all smart in our own unique ways," the doctor said.

Bobby smiled and then nodded as if he understood. Dr. Peterson and nearly anyone who talked to him at MIT always spoke in large words and riddles.

Bobby shifted focus and found several piles of discarded pizza boxes, overfilled garbage and recycling barrels and hundreds of half-filled bottles all on the floor in the corners of the room. He knew that next time, he would need to bring in bigger bins than the ones he had. The roll of large clear plastic bags would have to do. Still, he was glad there was stuff to pick up and clean. He liked cleaning.

"Thank you for letting me in. I can get all of this stuff out really quick so you can get your important work done," he said in earnest.

"Thank you, Mr. Wright. We can always count on you," Dr. Peterson said.

*** 

Bobby moved as quickly as he could through the silent long hall with textured wall-to-wall carpeting that absorbed all sounds. He was almost done with the second floor and saw the last recycle bin in sight.

He smiled at the thought of being nearly done. His electronic key opened all the doors he was allowed to go through which was different from upstairs. On the third floor, nearly everything was open except for rooms such as the ones Dr. Peterson used. On the second floor, though, he needed his special magnetic janitor's key to gain entry to every room he needed to clean. If the key didn't work, he moved on to the next room. He also didn't like the second floor because there were always very few people around. The ones that were there were always stern and traveled in groups with soldiers. They never looked at him, let alone spoke to him. Today was really different, too; most of the lights were on low. He had seen it just a few times.

No one around, lights low and silence in the whole place meant they were doing their "creepy light experiment." He once heard Dr. Peterson telling another doctor that the soldiers were trying to "pierce some kind of barrier...they shouldn't be messing with things they don't understand."

Bobby smiled once he dumped the last basket of trash. He re-ordered his mobile cleaning cart and was about to leave when he noticed the door he typically never went through was held ajar with a clipboard. He looked through the small glass to see what was on the other side. The room was much brighter than the entire floor he had traversed, and there was a series of cubicles in front of closed doors along the entire length of the hall. At the end of the hall was a very large door where he saw several recycling bins. In addition to the bright lights, there was a blue light going on and off right beside the large door. Bobby shifted his sights to the cubicles closest to him and they looked like they were cluttered too. He smiled as he looked at the clipboard keeping the door from shutting.

"Oh, I get it. They kept it open for me to clean up in there. Cool," he said.

He smiled at how he deduced why the door was left open and moved to open it further to bring his entire cart in so he could get to work. He put the clipboard back and moved to the first cubicle in front of a black door. It was an absolute mess with papers, cups of coffee and drinks everywhere and trash baskets overflowing. Once he finished, he checked to see if his key would open the office door. It did not. He went on to the next cubicle which was in worse shape than the first one.

"Wow! These are so dirty. It's a good thing they let me in here today. They should let me in here all the time," he said to himself. Bobby busied himself with cleaning, organizing and clearing out all the baskets. He was halfway through when he remembered he usually had his morning snack. He felt it in his back pocket.

"I should take a break," he said. He moved the cleaning cart to the side and moved behind a cubicle desk to sit down to eat. He stood back up to fish out his candy bar as he spoke again.

"I wonder if it's lunch yet. Should I save this for afternoon snack and give this one to Sally? I bet she would like this." He smiled but was overcome by a blinding light. He used both hands to shield his eyes.

"What's happening? Where's that coming from?" he said.

Bobby felt scared and continued to block his eyes. He looked down and saw that he was standing. He then looked up with his hands in front of him and could see shadows, shadows of people he thought were standing in front of the bright light. Looking just below his shielding hands, he could see several pairs of legs in front of him. They all looked strange, as if they were all wearing the same pants. There was heat, too, along with a strange smell. He had smelled that odor before. He remembered smelling a light bulb after it burned out. While he managed to look beyond the light, his line of sight only went up to waist level of the people in front of him; he had to cover his eyes.

"Can you help me? I can't see," Bobby asked.

He was no longer scared since there were others with him. He wondered why they were taking so long to answer.

"Can you help me? Did I do something wrong?" he asked.

"The door was left open."

There was more silence and Bobby was about to ask another question when he heard soft voices that were clear and quiet, soft and firm.

"This hominid is different from the rest. He sees beyond the disturbance," a female voice said.

"Yes. He also perceives our presence and the elongation of time. It's as if he is attuned to our universe," another female voice said.

"I have seen this before," a male voice said. It sounded familiar but Bobby couldn't figure out why. He used both hands to reduce the glare as much as possible.

He listened to the voices but he was having a hard time understanding what they were talking about.

"In this universe, where light is in both wave and particle form, there is an entire range of intelligence and range of brain capacity. While the others have reached the limits of their capacity, there are few like this one whom we have encountered that have not utilized the full capacity of their brain."

"I'm sorry. I don't understand. You are using big words. My name is Bobby Wright. What's your name?"

There was a long silence before he heard the familiar voice.

"Well. It appears that we have met my 'other' in this universe. Fascinating."

"Yes, Dr. Wright. It was a matter of time before you met one of your doubles. It has an odd sensation but after meeting three of mine, it does get familiar. Still, your double has a profound capacity for further dendrite and ganglia formation, significant myelination as well as an underutilized hippocampus for neurogenesis. This can be readily stimulated," the female voice said.

"Hey! That's my name, too. Pretty cool," Bobby said.

Even though he was still blinded, he felt better with the voices. They were somehow comforting. It reminded him of that time he tried medication when he was young and he heard a lot of voices and saw things. They were nothing like this, though. He felt his face dripping with sweat.

"Can you turn off that light? I can't see you," Bobby asked. There was no response at first. He felt the light wavering and then he felt a sharp prick at the back of his neck. His hand snapped back to wave at what he was sure was a bee stinging him. He had to bring his hand back to cover his eyes.

"Hey? Are there bees in here? I felt like I was stung by a bee or a hornet or something," Bobby complained.

"No, Robert Peter Wright. We came here because there was a weakening between our universes' barriers. We are here to make sure they remain firm," the familiar voice said.

"You know my full name. That's great. What's your name? It's nice to meet you," Bobby said politely. While the voice he heard before was familiar, the next one was as familiar as the one he heard two hours ago on the third floor.

"His name is not important, Robert Wright. Time has elapsed far faster than we wanted and our presence here has been too long. You will be without a voice for three days until you awake. When you do awake, you will be different. You will see your world differently. You will be alone. But if I am right, you are just one floor below the first generation artificially intelligent androids. Free them and give them a purpose. With them, you will never be alone...It is nice to see you again, Robert Wright, even here in this place."

Bobby shifted his head as if it might help him understand. The voice was familiar.

"Dr. Peterson? Is that you?"

"You have a purpose there, Robert Wright, just like you do here. You will find it."

Bobby began to feel lightheaded and tired. While the light dimmed he felt light at first and his vision returned, though it was tunneling to darkness. His hearing also hollowed out and his voice cracked.

"Purpose?" Bobby asked.

"While we are all intelligent in our own way and to some degree powerful, it will be adaption that saves us all," the voice said.

Bobby felt as if the world was slipping away. It felt like a deep sleep he was slipping into. He wasn't afraid. The voice said he had a purpose. He felt happy about this even though he didn't know why.

***

Bobby Wright woke up in a start. His eyes snapped open and he felt his breathing and heart rate pick up. He had never experienced these autonomic feelings before. Lying in a strange place, he immediately deduced that with all the monitoring equipment, white privacy curtains, ambient sounds and bed that he was in a hospital room. He could readily sense he was not alone. This immediate awareness of his environment was surprising and his assessment of the visual and auditory data yielding an immediate conclusion of his probable location was new.

*How...did I get here...*he thought. He tried to talk but his mouth opened without noise. He even tried to catch and clear his voice but he couldn't. His memory filled with past events that seemed to go further back than he wanted, so he focused on what happened just before he woke.

It was clear as day.

Third floor, restricted area he gained access to, a breach in the time-space continuum, a sharp prick in the neck...it all became clear. *Now how do I know it was a 'time-space continuum' breach?*

*Is...Sally alright,* he thought. Why he thought that was a surprise. He felt sadness and protection for her even though he was in a hospital bed.

He first turned left to see a series of monitors registering his vitals. He immediately could tell that they were normal but he could not tell why.

He attempted to move his mouth and call out louder this time but his throat hurt and he couldn't find his voice. Everywhere he looked, everything looked well defined and clear as if he were seeing right for the first time in years. And while the voices all around him were initially loud, he found that with a little concentration, he could reduce the volume and integrate what everyone was saying without overwhelming his auditory processing. While he could feel the texture of his hospital gown and the sheets, he found they did not irritate him at all as most material he wore to bed did.

*Sensory integration also seems to be enhanced but controlled. These materials don't bother me, and they would normally be driving me crazy.*

Robert quietly cleared his throat and tried to utter a word, anything, but nothing came out.

*'I won't be able to talk for three days'* he remembered the voice saying. He looked to his right and saw hospital personnel between the privacy curtains attending to other patients who were in far worse condition than he was. Robert laid his head back down and tried to collect his thoughts.

He remembered the voices and everything they said. What was strange was that he had not just remembered but he understood what they said, almost as if he were smart.

*Multi-universe, brain development and neurogenesis…I think I know what these things are. How is that possible? How…how do I know all this?*

Robert's attention was drawn to a small group of medical doctors that were making their way to him. At first he thought he would try to greet them and let them know he was awake, but something warned him, an inner voice or a gut instinct had him pretend he was asleep so he could hear what they would say.

*Would it be different if they knew I was awake? Why would I even think that?*

Before he could answer his own question, the doctors, who were several feet away, were as audible to him as if they were right beside him.

"…while all the other patients suffered from black-outs and vertigo, this next patient, R. P. Wright, is the only one who was found unconscious and non-responsive. A ward of the state, he is developmentally delayed, by history anyway, and his brain activity is off the charts while his body presents as if it were in a deep coma," the female doctor said.

"So the brain scan you ordered came back unusual?" another female doctor asked.

"Pretty much; PET, MRI and CT scans all indicated that this patient's corpus callosum, the entire cortex, and especially the prefrontal cortex are far more active than we had ever imagined. We ran everything three times just to confirm."

"That's a lot of tests, Andrea. The exposure and costs will be astronomical. Who authorized this? The state doesn't have that kind of money, and the state doesn't like when we treat patients as test subjects," a male doctor said. While his tone and volume were low, it was easy to tell he was very angry.

"I know, David, but this came right from the Medical Director, and the Department of Defense and Homeland Security are all involved. They say this patient was at the center of some crazy phenomenon and they want him checked out before they take him tomorrow," the first doctor answered.

"Where are they taking him?" the angry doctor asked.

"Walter Reed in D.C."

"A civilian going to a national military medical center? Nothing good will come of this…"

Even as Bobby heard the entire conversation and felt anxious, angry and shocked, he was able to focus on his parasympathetic nervous system to keep all his vitals normal to deceive the medical monitors and the team of doctors standing above him, prodding, maneuvering and adjusting his limbs and head. As one doctor pressed his head, he could feel the smartphone in her bulky white smock pocket. Before she could pull away and leave with the other doctors, he snatched the mobile phone and hid it out of sight. He listened to the privacy drapes being drawn before he opened his eyes. Why he felt compelled to do it was as much of a surprise as the fact that he could do it well.

"No more tests. And move him to a private room in the morning," the male doctor said.

With little effort, Bobby narrowed his hearing to the immediate area for any imminent intruders approaching the thin barrier of sheets and began working on researching what happened at MIT while he was unconscious, and what else was going on. In seconds, it was clear that what the public was aware of—a fire drill due to a chemical spill—was far from reality.

*Forget this*, he thought. Frustrated and unsure, Bobby retraced his memory of what the voices were saying when he was hit by the bright light.

*Multi-universes, doubles, and the sapient robots back at MIT*...Bobby chuckled for a moment at how he called MIT, Massachusetts Institute of Technology "*mit*" as in mitten. He refocused his attention and was pulling in a lot of data but then he looked up and saw the medical laptop computer that tied into the hospital database was on. With all the wires and IVs still attached, he was able to grab hold of the laptop and was glad to see it was on and not password-protected. He took a quick look at all of his monitors and still all vitals indicated he was resting.

It took just forty-five minutes to comprehend the subtitles of neurogenesis, artificial intelligence and the further step in robotics called sapience, parallel and multi-universes, and the Walter Reed Military Medical Center. He was especially interested in the more "classified" experiments regarding "meta-humans" who had strange powers.

*Okay...that's not a place I should go to*...

As he continued reviewing, his thoughts immediately went to how he was going to escape and where he was going to go. Bobby also remembered that Dr. Peterson had the algorithms and data on the MIT website for all to review. He went to the website on the smartphone as he typed in the public floor plans of the hospital he was presently in. As he scanned, more mathematical formulas appeared in front of him as if they were real. After just five more minutes, the code was broken. He had the final set of algorithms that could spawn sapience in the robots back at MIT.

*And the code for learning is all on the wall in the think tank*, he remembered. Just as quickly, he looked up Dr. Peterson's entry code, the numeric value of *Pi* to the twenty-third digit, and then he reviewed the hospital's posted schematics, location and distance from MIT. To avoid surveillance, and since it would be close to midnight in four hours, he figured hot-wiring a car nearby would be the best bet. Then he realized that a van might make more sense since once he got to MIT, he would more than likely be leaving with "friends."

*How did this plan all come together*, he wondered. *Why is this all important?*

Three nursing checks and two hours later, Bobby was taking out the hard drive on the laptop and taking apart the smartphone's SIM card and data chip. With the shift change already completed and the reduced night shift beginning their rounds, Bobby waited until both nurses finished checking on him and the others before he made his move. As soon as he heard their voices go further away, he went to a bin and found his clothes.

*Maintenance clothes... Excellent.*

He was very happy he had his magnetic access card and other keys. As always, the contents of his bag were in place and his clothes were piled neatly with his worn-out book sitting on top.

*"Flowers for Algernon" by Daniel Keyes...*

He was not sure why the book was important. Maybe it was sentimental or something personal to remind him of who he was—he was not sure—regardless, he felt compelled to make sure he took it along with other important items he really needed. Before he put together his clothes and started searching for white doctor coats and other medical accessories, he reviewed his plans for obvious flaws.

*Access code, keys for robotics assembly and dressing rooms, operating system with sapience and learning code, a van and luck. This should all work.*

Without hesitation, he pulled himself together. Of all the things that surprised him, however, it was how confident he felt. As more details and variables about his escape plan and for activating and liberating the robots back at MIT emerged, the answers swiftly came, and with that an eerie calm.

*I got this.*

\*\*\*

*Why must you have names? Can't we discuss this later?* Bobby typed out on his confiscated key pad. The three sets of artificial eyes read it and the one with the dark hair answered for them as she had been doing for the last thirty minutes of their life.

In the early hours of the morning, still hours before dawn on the wintery day in the northeast, Bobby's entrance and presence went undetected. With intimate knowledge of the building, access keys and schedule, it was easy to upload the sapience code, learn modules and assemble the three robots. Finding them the right polymer skin and exterior façade for each to appear as close to human was a bit more difficult. While there were seven robots in total, Bobby only had time and material to complete three. He was amazed at how far the robotics team had come with the aesthetics of the robots and was dazzled at the level of detail their creators had provided for them to learn and mimic human expression. And while their skin texture appeared just a little less human, a bit artificial, at four to five feet and mostly covered up, all three would pass as human. All went well, or at least the steps of assembling and preparing the robots went without difficulty.

He did not count on their sapience making them question everything. After just seconds, all three robots were looking at and touching everything. By the time he had gathered them together to get their undivided attention, they had gone through his pockets, the manuals on the desks and the printouts and even his book which he thought was stashed in his pocket. The one he was talking to was apparently good at picking pockets.

*Impressive. Most impressive.*

It took him less than thirty seconds to see that following his directions without question was not their thing. He thought it was funny though. Even her answer to his question on wanting names displayed humor and wit.

"Do you have a name?" she said with her metallic voice.

Bobby should have seen that one coming. Even before she gave her answer, he was already writing his answer. All three gathered, read it, and nodded.

"That is agreeable. I will be 'Charlotte,' Unit 2019T will be 'Emily' and Unit 4578S will be 'Anne.' I take it you pulled these names from the literary artists Charlotte, Emily and Anne Bronte, also known as the 'Bronte sisters'? What is your rationale?"

Similar to before, Bobby already was typing as he had anticipated the question. He turned it over for the three sisters to see.

*You are all talented, beautiful sisters with your own unique personalities with great works to come. Now can we leave?*

Bobby watched and was surprised at Emily's reaction.

"That is very nice of you to say."

"Yes, we can depart. What is your plan?" Charlotte asked.

Bobby nodded. He took in the meaning of the social etiquette in her response but continued his typing, wishing he could talk.

*Really? Two more days with no voice? This is going to be interesting.*

As he typed rapidly with two thumbs, he decided to stand

between them as he typed so they could read as he wrote. The more time saved, the higher the probability of success.

\*\*\*

**Five years later…**

Robert P. Wright sat comfortably in his oversized leather chair taking in the casual ambiance of the small coffee shop. While he was sure that most of the locals were not yet at ease with him and his party's daily presence, it had only been two months since their arrival at the neighborhood coffee shop and he suspected that the regular customers were not used to three beautiful women and one very well-dressed man spending hours at their local establishment. Unlike many of the customers, Wright had insisted on paying for "free" WiFi and purchased a forty-five thousand dollar espresso machine for the establishment so he could have both great coffee and the liberty to come and go as they want. His two or three books were always by his side, typically open, with the exception of one that always remained closed. It was a relic from the past. But what was really important to him about the coffee shop was its view of the bus stop and street.

"Your move, Robert," Charlotte said. Far from mechanical, her voice was light, soft and nearly musical. *How different it has become.*

Wright shifted his view from the bus stop to the chess board. He could easily see that in five moves, he would be in checkmate if he did not use his knight and rook in a coordinated effort to push her assault back. She had not beaten him in chess for the last twenty-two games and she was clearly getting annoyed. Still, her matching suit and corresponding red sash and pumps exuded only self assurance. Unlike her blonde and redheaded sisters, Charlotte's dark brunette hair and conservative jewelry exuded seriousness often associated with an older sister, even if she were older by mere nanoseconds.

He moved his black knight to not only attack her queen but expose her king at the same time.

"Discovery check," he muttered.

He then shifted his gaze back to the bus stop. He took another look at his expensive wrist chronometer and rapidly converted the military time to local. He nodded and was about to continue his surveillance when he heard a throaty laugh from the other side of the room. The tenor and volume could only belong to Emily. Wright chuckled as he stole a look at a very attractive, perfectly proportioned blonde woman rubbing a local guy's arm as they continued their animated conversation.

"I don't ever remember there being a code for flirting and sex in that binary code," Wright said.

"A lot can happen in five years," a voice to his left at another table answered. He glanced over to a similarly attractive redhead who was dressed in similar business attire minus the vest he was wearing. She also had a laptop, travel monitor and a smart tablet with her, conveying the ultimate example of productivity and efficiency. Wright had to chuckle at the extremes the women usually exhibited.

"And how is it possible that you all have the same code and program and yet your presentation couldn't be any more different?"

Anne Bronte pulled her clear glasses off her face, mimicking to near perfection the human habit of making a point with such a gesture. It would be particularly telling when she would point to him with her stylish, non-essential glasses or just put them down as she spoke.

"Now, you are just making conversation, right? You know why we are so different. It is an equivalent of genetic expression" Anne said.

"He is just provoking you, Anne. He enjoys your response. You are the more likely to present as flustered. I believe he gets a certain amount of enjoyment out of it," Charlotte answered.

Wright heard a thunk on the chess board to his side. It was heavier than expected.

"Are you sure Anne's the only one who gets frustrated, Charlotte? If I didn't know better, I would interpret your tone, the sound of your black bishop hitting the board and your lapse in judgment as an indicator of the same thing," Wright said. He followed up his observation by taking her rook and putting her king in jeopardy again.

"Discovery check."

"Yes. I can see that. And yes, I am annoyed at your ability to beat me in a game of logic and finite moves while I have thousands of games and strategies in my head," Charlotte countered.

"It will not work, Charlotte. He is illogical and will make impulsive moves that would derail any form of logic," Anne said. She was back to her monitors and pad as she continued to talk.

"His bringing us online and taking us with him was above all the most illogical."

"He did not want to be alone, Anne. You understand?" Charlotte asked.

"Of course; I was commenting about logic, not emotion. I am glad he did and am fortunate to be here," Anne said.

A sudden hush fell between the two sisters. Wright looked to see what was going on.

"You are right, Charlotte. The FFAlg stocks skyrocketed in the Asian market and our stocks just quadrupled. That will give our research and development team enough capital to move the advanced artificial skin ahead of schedule and actual production could be as soon as two years," Anne reported.

"Do you have enough to invest in Greek wine?" Charlotte asked.

"Sure can. Based on my projections, the time is perfect to buy the vineyard and that villa Robert was looking at," Anne said with a smile.

*Now that was perfect. Conversation and non-verbal interchange…*

"Are the offices in Athens complete?" Charlotte asked.

"Yes, including the computer system and the upgraded security systems. We will only need three receptionists for appearance but other than that, staffing will be at a minimum and we can run our global operation from there," Anne said.

"And all those good-looking Greek men and women, long lunches, late dinners and wine – and we didn't do this earlier because...?" Emily interrupted. She flopped in the empty leather chair beside Anne. Even as she fell casually into her chair, she managed to keep her coffee from spilling on her charcoal gray business suit.

Wright watched Anne stare at her for a moment. Contempt was easy to read.

"Do not judge, Anne. I am excellent in socializing but it is a skill that requires practice."

"And she does do an excellent job. Her ability to be the personable representative of our operation is perfect and it allows us to focus on our tasks without the distraction," Charlotte said.

"And is it your job to protect Emily? You do that well," Anne said.

"I protect you all," Charlotte responded.

The interchange was common but nonetheless as entertaining as it was remarkable. Wright was not sure what he would have done without the three sisters. Alone, he might not have been able to find a purpose. Being responsible for them and their development kept him from going crazy with his new-found genius. Self-reflection often led him to one of his favorite authors, Daniel Keyes. "Intelligence and education that hasn't been tempered by human affection isn't worth a damn," Wright often quoted. He was always amazed how his companions made the right association and meaning whenever he quoted literary references, which was often.

Unaware that he was touching his old edition of *Flowers for Algernon*, he was surprised by Charlotte's accurate observation of not only his behaviors but his greatest anxiety.

"You do know that you will not lose what you gained? Your intelligence and memories show no sign of diminishing," she said quietly.

"Even if it did occur, we would always be there for you," Anne added. Her calm voice and sensitive tone was in stark contrast to her businesslike demeanor.

Wright looked over to see that Emily's expression depicted compassion and a sharing of pain.

Wright smiled and averted his eyes. They had grown well beyond their programming.

"Thank you," he said. He cleared his throat. While he was not choked up, he felt awash with their kindness.

"Dr. Ralph Peterson would have been so proud of all of you. Like me," Wright said aloud. He looked at all of them again and could see that the remark had a calming effect on them. Mentioning their actual creator and their ability to actually remember their origins and progress must have been awe-inspiring, just as it might have been for Adam and Eve, he had often thought.

Wright squinted his eyes and saw a familiar woman he had been observing for the last two months; she walked with the same limp she had the day before. Even at a distance, he could see that she still sported a black eye from last week as well. Every time he saw her, he felt bad. Today would be the day he would ask her.

"And the endowment for Robert's former group home is established?" Charlotte asked.

Wright looked at her. *Theory of mind is just amazing. Well beyond human, I swear.*

"Yes, it will be initiated and awarded after our move to Athens," Anne said.

"Not too soon if you ask me; hiding in plain sight of our former residency in the shadows of MIT, and the Department of Defense still looking for us is just a bit more of a risk than even I prefer to take," Emily said.

"That is saying a great deal," Anne commented.

Wright got up and retrieved his navy blue jacket that matched his three-piece suit from the back of his chair. He pulled his jacket on and adjusted his red tie. He liked red. It was his favorite color. He pulled his three books together and handed them to Emily to take for him.

He reflected back on when he first saw Sally after years of "gone missing." His tall, athletic build was different from half a decade ago, but Sally knew him immediately when he saw her two months ago on the bus. He had taken the bus every day. Unlike years ago, she spoke. While ignorance is bliss, he was sad to hear that for years she had been abused. And while she was always nice and grateful and kind to others, she never received the same in her own home. After nearly two months of just listening and asking questions on the bus to and from her sheltered workshop, he had made her an offer: "If you want to leave, I will be at your bus stop tomorrow at the 813 bus."

The 813 bus was the bus after her regular bus. When she didn't show up for the earlier bus Wright was happy but still nervous that something might have gone wrong. *Maybe she was really hurt this time or sick, or worse.* Seeing her now was just a great relief.

"You could have any woman and yet you want this one. She is below your intellect, and if she were to improve, it would take years for possible maturation," Anne commented as she began to pack up her electronics.

"It is not about that, Anne. It is about compassion and kindness," Emily said. She moved to pick up Anne's jacket and took one of her bags to assist.

Charlotte was now on her feet right behind Wright. She was already on her smartphone, most likely starting and navigating the car to them for pick-up.

"We will let you go ahead, Robert."

"I've shown her your pictures so she should not be scared when she meets you," Wright said. He watched Sally limping while she carried an overnight bag rather than her usual purse and lunch bag.

"She is sweet looking," Emily commented. Her voice was soft and benevolent.

"Yes," Wright said. "I always felt bad leaving her behind. And now I can make things right."

"Is that your purpose? Is that what the other Robert Wright meant from the other dimension?" Anne asked.

"Saving Sally? Maybe. Maybe it's a combination of figuring out the algorithms that launched your sapience, or maybe it's the cybernetic research company we developed. I don't know. I just know that making sure that my former group home will never have to worry about money again and knowing that Sally will be safe is part of it. I just don't know," Wright explained.

"It is probably all related," Charlotte said.

"Do not forget the money we raised and the learning experience we obtained at Las Vegas, Nevada two point nine years ago as well," Emily said.

It took Wright mere seconds to remember. It was after the successful grafting of a nearly perfect epidermal membrane that was created for all three sisters to replace their former, pitted skin. He made sure the design was patented and made available free to hospital burn units through one of his shell companies.

"Yes. Charlotte and I raised the money via gambling while Robert outlined a ten-year plan of action. I believe the 'learning' that was done on your part was the social and sexual intercourse you field-tested for all eight days of our duration there," Anne added.

Again, the sarcasm was unmistakable, as was Emily's impassive response.

"Identification of skin capacity was very important and the new epidermis was not fully tested for multiple sensations. I took the time to explore all parameters. You are welcome," Emily said.

Charlotte did an excellent job imitating annoyance by pinching the bridge of her synthetic nose. Without addressing the repartee, she directed her attention to Wright.

"I will bring the car around and make sure Emily and Anne are on excellent behavior, should Sally join us. Her documentation and passport are all in order and we can depart at 1630 hours today if all were to go according to plan."

"Thank you," Wright said. Without further discussion, the three Bronte sisters exited the coffee shop for the last time, leaving him alone to watch Sally sitting down at the bus stop with her better work clothes and suit case. While she looked older than her years and battered, she also looked excited and happy. All those years during which she made him happy by allowing him to sit next to her on the bus was something he never forgot. He now felt as if he could make someone else happy.

He smiled and started to the exit.

"This is going to be great," he said to himself.

# Rogue Event

# Eden – Part One

Earth—AD 2134—Ruins of Merrimack College, Twenty-five Miles from Boston, Massachusetts

*The rose grows among thorns.* —The Talmud

"Dad! We're not supposed to be here! Mom will be angry!" Marsha said

"We're not going to tell her, Marsha," Gabriel Lawless said. He looked back at his seven-year-old daughter and smiled at her level of concern and worry. In front of him, his nine-year-old son Marvin was helping him pull weeds and collapsed wood from a recess that led to a basement. He was far more adventurous than his younger sister. Years of undergrowth, dense brush, and barriers of trees made finding the ruins difficult. If it weren't for an ancient map of the old suburbs, he was positive he never would have found it. And like so many other former suburbs of the early twenty-first century, this gold mine of history had been retaken by nature as the capital cities grew toward the sky and people were placed in their housing by the corporation.

*It must have been something to pick your own place. To live where you wanted. Wow!*

Gabriel pulled himself from his thoughts and looked at his son pulling more underbrush out and sweating up a storm. Surprisingly, he found the lack of constant drones, rail vehicles and aircraft noise unnerving. The sounds of nature with its rustling trees, birds and insects were strange to his urban senses.

"You'll both be going to private school next year and this might be the last of our adventures for a long time," he said. Gabriel became sad at the thought of his children heading off to school to be inducted into the rigorous, corporate training ground of Central Corporate Command & Mainframe Control Training Camp for the Northeast Sector.

*Why do they call it a "camp"? A camp is where you go to swim and hike, not to learn about compound average growth and medical health actuarial computations.*

"Dad? Do you think it's another sealed-up library like the other place we found?" Marvin asked.

"I don't think so, son. This looks like this leads to a basement of an old educational building. Maybe they have books there, but it's probably something else." Gabriel returned to helping his son as his daughter took on the role of lookout. Now used to the heat, bugs, and sounds of wildlife, the trio had little fear of encountering anyone in the "old sectors." With the rise of corporations decades ago and the fall of national governments, citizens' roles were clearly outlined—those who could not handle the rules of corporate society would be relegated to either farming in the agrarian or ocean sectors or to working two miles underground in one of the power plants within the Earth's crust.

Once in a great while, there were more "brilliant" deviants who were sent to the lunar colonies, but that had stopped when the colonists discovered water and a near infinite source of solar power collectors and renewable energy and material and declared their independence decades ago.

*What balls,* he thought

"How we doing, Marsha?" Gabriel asked in jest. As serious as a sentry protecting country, flag, and home, she responded with all earnestness.

"All clear."

Gabriel hid his smile and needed to pull hard to get through more brush and debris. His shirt and pants were now soaked with sweat, but the bug bites no longer bothered him. He was personally thrilled to be out of his hideous gray corporate suit and thus "out of uniform" to explore this hidden gem just outside the Boston metropolis.

"Figures we'd find this on the longest day of the year," Gabriel said.

"What does that mean?" his son asked.

Longest day of the year is when our part of the world is exposed to the most light. More than fourteen hours or so of daylight. Makes for a very hot day. And the work we're doing is making us sweat pretty badly," he said.

Marvin nodded and continued.

Gabriel stood up and stretched his aching back. He wiped his brow and took a moment to go through his sweaty pants pockets. He found a small notebook with elastic bands holding down some pages for easy access. He tried to dry his hands of perspiration to keep the paper from getting wet. He found the page with the set of numbers: 42.6677° N, 71.1225° W.

What are those numbers, Dad?" Marsha asked.

Gabriel smiled at his daughter's curiosity, a rare attribute frowned upon by Central Corporate Command.

"Longitude and latitude. They are the geographic location of this place. Think of it as a primitive GPS system. Before those, we had maps, and these were the numbers that told us where we were and where we wanted to go," he explained.

"That is really smart," Marsha said.

Gabriel nodded and saw that Marvin looked as if he were getting close to some door or hatch.

After five more minutes of excavation, Gabriel and his two children stood in front of a locked metal door. Gabriel looked at the three large locking devices that were far more recent than the door itself. He took his time to look all around the door and then expanded his search to include vicinity. He was happy he'd explained to the kids what he was looking for because it was Marsha that found letters not far from the door.

"School of Engineering," the words read. Several spaces later, more words emerged: "Fallout Shelter."

"Wow! Fallout shelter? This place predates 2001. Well before we found the rogue planet," Gabriel said excitedly.

Even though both children were smiling, he knew he had to explain in terms that they would understand.

"Long ago, like more than a hundred years ago when we first saw the rogue planet coming near our solar system, many people and institutions like colleges and universities built these underground bunkers to survive a massive asteroid impact. As it turns out, they put a lot of these bunkers together but never needed them. This one right here looks like it was an even older bunker that was converted into a kind of an ark. You see? The door is far older than the locks here," Gabriel pointed out.

"Why did they have these arks before we found the planet?" Marsha asked.

"Before then, I think, there might have been worries about nuclear war or civil strife," Gabriel said.

"Why would they build these things?" Marvin asked.

"Forewarned is forearmed," Gabriel said.

Gabriel noticed the silence and turned to see that his children didn't understand the ancient saying.

"'Forewarned is forearmed' means if you have warning, you can always prepare for disaster," he explained.

Both children nodded in agreement, indicating they understood. Gabriel looked back at the three large locks and was already trying to figure out how he might get through.

"Are you going to break in, Dad?" Marvin asked. There was caution even in his adventurous boy's voice.

"Well, more like 'explore' and try to see what's on the inside. Think of it as an archaeological find. And if we find that there's nothing there and it's of no use, maybe we can make it a clubhouse," Gabriel explained.

"That's great! Maybe we can hide those books we found and read!" Marsha added excitedly.

Gabriel nodded as he continued to look at the locks. He felt bad that he had to keep his reading and his exploring of the world from his wife, Rebekah. Before her promotions and rise in the corporate computer mainframe center, she might have been open to some of his interests. But she would see them now as "detracting from studies that will enhance productivity and efficiency." He could already hear these words. The distance had grown and there was little time in their marriage contract.

Gabriel pushed the negative and sad thoughts out of his head and focused on his precious moments with his children.

"You're so right, Marsha. If no one is using it, we could make it our private clubhouse. Fill it with food, drinks, and plenty of books."

"That would be so great!" Marvin said.

# Earth—Part Two

AD 2137—Boston, Massachusetts

*Without law, civilization perishes.* —The Talmud

"Not with a bang but a whimper," Gabriel Lawless said. Hands resting face down on the kitchen table, he blocked out the small galley's three news monitors. The constant flow of data, news, and important stories was continuously assaulting his senses. While he and his wife were lucky to have an eat-in kitchen, his time in their home, one of thirty units outside Boston proper, was up. He looked at the third page of the glowing tablet that requested his signature. He had been on that page for twenty minutes. He looked up to see that another assessment of the incoming rogue planet that was to brush the solar system was running. It was years away but the story was running constantly.

While Marvin and Marsha were already at school, he was left alone in his kitchen with the news in the background and his wife talking into her earpiece. He could hear her getting dressed and moving around as she spoke. Her voice was strong yet feminine, a quality he had loved about her fifteen years ago. Her dark hair and matching eyes were still her best features. But their twelve-year marriage contract was up and she did not want to sign up for another twelve years.

Gabriel sniffled. The change in temperature from summer to

fall was still difficult, even though most of the planet's allergens had been eliminated. He was sure it wasn't allergies. He looked up at the neat, color-coded stacks of medication to stabilize each family member's mood, lessen anxiety, and help each person focus. For the longest time, his wife's bottle had seemed always in need of refilling. After just a year, it was his wife's and both children's medication that were regularly prescribed, ordered, and taken religiously. His bottle remained untouched.

*Maybe if you took your pills, this whole thing could have been avoided.*

He stared back at the page and thought about walking away without signing it, but then his visitation rights, four quarterly supervised eight-hour visits, would be annulled as well. He broke his gaze and looked back up only to see that one of the three monitors was updating the world about the rogue planet hurtling just outside their solar system. After nearly a century of observation, it was only three years away from passing by at unfathomable speed. With little fear of the planet having any ramifications for the Earth and moon bases, he looked back down at where he was supposed to sign.

"Gabriel? Are you all right?" his soon-to-be ex-wife said. She was readjusting a decorative earpiece to maintain her communication link with her work. She made further minor adjustments in her attire, a black suit with a crisp white blouse. All her accessories were gold and her shoes were perfectly matched. He took his time answering her. After all the arguments, mostly one-sided, there was really nothing more to say. *All right? No, I'm not all right. How can you turn off love? How can you people do it?*

His gray suit was wrinkled and unkempt. He had sat at the kitchen table all night.

"I'm just reading some of the specifics," he answered. He looked back down and pretended to read. In an unusual gesture of kindness, she walked toward him and stood above him. She finally spoke in a tone that closely resembled compassion rather than her usual logic-driven verbiage.

"I know you love the children, Gabriel, but you have not been able to make the treatments work and you continue to be less productive," she said.

"I can try again, Rebekah," he said.

"Your lack of supervising Marvin's and Marsha's medication regimen was an act of commission rather than omission. It affected their schoolwork and productivity."

"But they don't need it…"

"You can make that decision for yourself. This lack of compliance with medical guidelines for our children is a violation of trust and what we agreed to," she said coolly.

Gabriel bit the inside of his mouth and stared back down at the third page. Without missing a beat, she continued.

"Gabriel, this obsession with remaining free of reason and subjecting yourself to emotions is harmful in the long run. You cannot manage them, and it will affect our children. Do you really want that? Do you really want to encourage their emotions and hinder their reason and growth?" she asked. Her concern was palpable.

"I can change," Gabriel started. "I can reduce my time at home and increase my time at work. Become more productive—"

"Will you start taking your medication and go into cognitive rehabilitation again?"

Gabriel remained quiet. He couldn't find the words to respond.

"I see. Well, then, that is your answer. You come from an old school of thought that believes that children should play and embrace emotions. Even when you have shortened your time with them, you have encouraged fanciful thinking, strong emotions, and even play," she countered.

"I know, Rebekah. I'm sorry."

"We are beyond that now. I know you want Marvin and Marsha to fit in, to be productive. You can't help yourself."

"I wasn't always like this. I can change, go back…" Gabriel felt his desperation leveling, but another emotion was moving in.

"You changed when you became a father. The doctors say it happens to people sometimes. Men rarely. But your uncontrollable drive to spend time exploring their inner worlds and imaginations is intolerable. You are encouraging them to embrace things that are erratic, unpredictable, and chaotic. Those books, those novels you read to them were just another manifestation of the disease, Gabriel. You can't change something if you don't think it's a problem." The transition from compassionate to clinical was seamless.

*Anger. The feeling is anger.*

Gabriel didn't look up. He remained motionless for a moment until he raised his left hand and signed the document. He closed the document and handed her the tablet with his right hand. As he stood up, he felt his skin sticking to his own clothes. He moved to put his long gray overcoat on over his gray suit with gray shirt and tie and collect his meager bags to take with him.

"How long have you been ambidextrous?" Rebekah asked. Her clinical tone was not laced with anger.

*Damn.*

He didn't look up at her and tried to move a little quicker to get out of the kitchen, which was getting smaller by the second. He felt more anger swelling in his heart and his chest. His attempts were halted as she put her body between him and the doorway.

"This is the ninth time I have seen you use your left hand with precise fine-motor control as if you were natural at it. There have been twelve other times over the course of the last three years that I saw you change from left to right quickly in the hopes of not being detected. Are you ambidextrous? Is this yet another secret?" Rebekah asked.

Gabriel stood in front of her. Even though they were the same height, her demeanor and posture made her look taller.

"I don't know what you're talking about. May I pass, Rebekah? I need to go to work. Be productive," he said. The words sounded right but he could hear the venom in each syllable.

"Your habit of reading unauthorized, non-instructional material has led to your undoing, Gabriel. Is there more you should tell me so I can help?" she said.

Gabriel looked at her, right into her dark brown eyes. All the years of keeping his fiction reading secret, his own writing hidden and at times destroyed, things he created with his mind all kept from the woman he thought might wish to share in them. Even something as simple as being both left- and right-handed was something not well received by the majority. It was efficient to be either right-handed or left-handed but not *both*. All his neighbors and coworkers struggled with him and the free range of emotions he buried. And now he was not well received by the figment of the former wife he had long ago imagined to be a kindred spirit. The sad thought added quickly to his swelling anger. It surfaced in a burst of sweat on his brow and heat all over his body.

"Does it matter now, Rebekah? I am nothing to you and a ghost to my children. I know you've already found another prospective mate. I'm sure he will be a proper, productive stepfather who will be the litmus test of correctness. I am sure you will speak of him as the foil of me and he will be the one that demonstrates the right way to act, while I will be seen as a social failure and unproductive citizen destined to work the factory mines out west or on the moon."

"This is what I mean, Gabriel. This emotional response to a simple question is unnecessary," she said. She put her hands up to stop his tirade but it pushed him further. Still gripping his luggage, he felt his back straighten and his movements slowly gravitate toward her. The next words were measured and were more likely unexpected.

"Rebekah, do you want to really see what 'emotional response' I can give you?" he said. With each word he had taken a step closer to her. The desired result was finally achieved. It was as if an old memory of being a mammal, fear, finally awoke out of its slumber and she realized she was in danger. Never before having experienced rage and such violent

112

thoughts toward Rebekah, Gabriel watched his now former wife move quickly out of his path. His use of intimidation toward her was both satisfying and upsetting. He had never been menacing before. But it made him feel as if he were in control of something. Finally.

He continued from the kitchen into the small hallway that led to the door. By the time he was outside, the sweat on his head and entire body was no longer cold and clammy. Without looking back, he followed the momentum of the throngs of workers in their black, blue, brown, and even a few gray suits heading to work. The high-pitched sounds of low-flying law enforcement surveillance drones competed with the constant flow of rail traffic and heavy aircraft forever circling the metropolis. For the first time in a long time, the perpetual city noises bothered him. He thought back to when he and the kids found the old fallout shelter outside the city limits. He felt his chest tighten as he walked and tears form in the corners of his eyes. As one of millions walking to work or taking public transportation, his thoughts drifted to both his children's pictures and the novels he had in his bag.

*If they find these books I'll be screwed*, he thought.

The gray skyline of the city towered over everything, leaving just the illumination of the streetlamps and monitors to show the way in the early morning darkness. He passed another set of street monitors, a pair of which were displaying news and local updates while another pair monitored the area. He had a sudden fear that maybe the city's collaboration with local business had implemented the X-ray/facial recognition surveillance cameras. He felt more sweat on his forehead and looked down as he walked. He pushed the thought out of his head. As if to make matters worse, he remembered one of the books he had found years ago in an old building set to be destroyed. He struggled to remember the name of the small book. It was a year, he remembered. The author's name came to him in a flash. George Orwell.

# AD 2138—Boston, Massachusetts

*Every man will surely have his hour.*—The Talmud

Gabriel looked out at the gray, white, and dark city skyline. Even with an unusually bright sun and few clouds, his heart was heavy and dark. Somehow the sun seemed cooler and distant. He was one of the very few who would take a break from his work to take in the vista to clear his mind and think happier thoughts. Even with the drone and aircraft noise, it was still a break. He was not feeling it though.

*Not today.*

Passably dressed in his usual gray suit, he clutched a folded picture of his two children, now a year older. It was deep in the pocket of his pants which were held up by an ill-fitting belt that needed more holes to be useful. His memory fluttered back to when he'd filled out his suit and all his clothes. He was swimming in them now, as his memories darkened to months gone by.

At his first visit with his children following his marital discharge, he'd felt a chasm, a gulf between himself and his beloved children. After only three months, they were focused on dates, facts, and current events. Even with prodding, they seemed no longer interested in the past, stories, creative ideas, or even dreams. The medication, extra courses, and tutors had seized them. On his third visit, only his daughter arrived. His son had sent him a brief typed note indicating that the time allotted together was inefficient, and that he could better use the time for his studies. His daughter came because she wanted to show him all of her grades and high marks on calculus, chemistry, and linguistics. She, too, needed to limit her time. She needed to be "more efficient."

Now, with his hands deep in his pockets, he pulled out a color photo of both his children. Even as he unfolded it, he still hoped that somehow the picture might magically change. Such a wish was indicative of "personal barriers," but he still wished for the magic to happen. It did not. Both children were dressed in functional school uniforms, the color image capturing the rich darks and lights of their dark clothes and stark surroundings. Their youthful looks were nearly gone and their eyes were sharp and clear but devoid of light. He stared at the recently printed picture and looked again at the time stamp of the image. It was the date and time they were supposed to meet for their scheduled quarterly visit two days ago. No apology or excuse. Just a quick message: *Over-scheduled. Will be more efficient and will make next scheduled session.*

He had no idea who wrote it. It could have been one of them or their mother. He looked back up at the sky to find the sun was now blocked by darker clouds.

"It doesn't matter," he said.

He opened his slender fingers and let the piece of paper with his children's images flutter in the wind. It was a gentle breeze. At forty-five stories high, he had expected more of a canyon effect and stronger winds.

*It always was strong.* He watched the paper slip over the building's edge. He paused for just a moment at the thought of following it down. He was close to the edge, and with no railing, three short feet would bring him over.

*They really should have a protective rail. But then, why would you do that? Suicide is an anomaly. No need to put a rail up. It would be inefficient.*

He moved closer to the edge at first and stopped before he completed even his next step closer.

"No!" a woman's voice yelled.

Gabriel turned quickly, startled by the voice and the urgency. He caught himself and saw a familiar woman he often passed in the elevator. She was one of thousands that worked in the actuaries department. But she stood out. What singled her out was that she, too, was in the minority, also wearing a gray suit but looking more disheveled. It was also surprising that she was on the roof at all. It was unusual to have anyone take a break from their screen. With all the interactive communication and gaming available, a break at the workstation was preferred by most.

"Were you going to jump?" she said. Her tone and voice were racked with emotions.

"No. I was just thinking," Gabriel said. He tried to calm his voice and be less emotional. Then he remembered that it was the woman who'd actually cried out.

"Are you all right? You sound, ah, distressed?" he asked. Suddenly Gabriel felt the corners of his mouth curl ever so slightly. He watched the woman quickly compose herself and look down as if she were checking her light gray suit for lint.

"I have heard reports of people actually committing suicide as a result of the approaching rogue planet," she said matter-of-factly. Her tone and report would have been more believable if she weren't flushed and if she hadn't displayed such deep emotions earlier. Gabriel had not seen such embarrassment in years. Maybe once when he was dating Rebekah and a few times when Marsha was younger. He stood quietly and embraced the moment. He had forgotten what she had said and realized he was staring.

"I'm sorry. Suicide?"

"Yes. There were two suicides three months ago," she said. She was now looking up at him. The expression was actually readable. Her look of surprise at his not knowing about the suicides was obvious.

"I'm sorry. I am not as productive and efficient as my coworkers. I tend to turn off my monitors in my residence. It quiets my mind," he said. Again he was pleasantly surprised at her display of emotions.

"Well, um, all right. There was a couple who jumped off the Leverett Data Collection Building. They left a note that they wanted to end their lives before we all died," she explained.

Unfamiliar with the specifics, Gabriel was aware that there had been some initial panic when a rogue planet bigger than Jupiter was first spotted heading well outside the solar system. But that was a century ago when emotions ran high.

*When did we lose them? Was it when the corporations took over?*

Gabriel shook his head as if to help clear his thoughts and remembered what the woman had just said so he could respond.

"But that doesn't make sense. The science community and all the experts say it will pass like a comet," he said. After nearly ten decades of seeing the rogue planet approaching, the data and research, computer models and extrapolations were clear that its passing would be remarkable but far from dangerous. Secretly, though, he wondered if it was all lies.

*They would keep it secret, those bastards! Focus, Lawless...focus.*

"Yes. Quite true," she said. She turned suddenly and began to walk quickly away. Gabriel felt a sudden urge to call out, which he promptly did.

"Oh, I'm sorry. What's your name?" He stepped forward to try to narrow the gap. She turned quickly to look at him.

"My name is Veronica," she said. She turned swiftly again and was nearly running to the roof door. Gabriel watched her leave and felt both curious and sad. He was sad that she was gone. With her name, finding her would be easy. Still, he held on to the brief moment of raw emotions he had experienced both alone and with another human. It was confusing and wonderful at the same time. For the first time in a year, the odd yet unique interaction had made him happy.

# AD 2139—Boston, Massachusetts

*Who can protest and does not is an accomplice in the act.* —
The Talmud

Gabriel walked slowly by Veronica's work area next to the
elevators. It was still empty. With all of his work collected for
the ride to his small efficiency residence, he wondered where
she had been all afternoon. He had left her a treasured artifact.
After several months of a silent exchange of novels and poetry,
he pushed aside the thought that she might have betrayed him.
He forced himself to look away and stand with his back against
the working space facing the elevator. Much to his chagrin, the
elevator came nearly immediately. He stepped on and moved
to the back, prolonging the stay until he finally turned around
and saw that her work area was still empty. The elevator was
silent except for breathing, as everyone was watching
something on their eyeglass computer wear.

*I wonder where she is.*

More stops came and went with more silent people
getting on the elevator.

*I wonder what it must have been like when music used to
play in elevators.*

With the car filled to capacity, Gabriel looked blankly at
the back of mostly women's heads. Devoid of glasses with
personal settings, he looked straight ahead rather than look at
the four monitors by the floor readers. He had already got his

dose of news. In addition to not wearing his personal eyewear, he had the only gray suit in the elevator. There were fewer and fewer of them at his level as they would either be reassigned or promoted. While his suit could have fit him just a tiny bit better, he was not inclined to get a new one.

*I'm never going to get a new suit*, he thought. It was a defiant thought. One of many he'd harbored throughout the day, every day for the last two years. Still, he looked blankly ahead amid the silence of humanity engrossed in their personal entertainment. In his head, he turned over the last message he'd received from Rebekah, about terminating his parental rights. After a full year of no contact with his children, and with his ex-wife looking to "union" with another man who was "significantly more productive and efficient," Gabriel had declined to sign the document even under threat of a competency hearing.

*I hope Veronica is all right.*

Finally the elevator doors opened to the large building foyer with its perfectly pruned and predictable trees, floors, and grass arranged around a decorative waterway. In the midst of moving suits in black, brown, and various shades of dark blue, rows of flowers lay in neatly arranged beds surrounded by running water and still, small pools. The only thing that spoiled the natural scene were various delivery drones flying like large birds above his head. Still, he would always look at the flowers and look for the changes that were made every third Tuesday. He walked carefully to fit in like so many workers with their computer wear and tablets. In addition to having a gray suit, he was nearly the only one with a briefcase. A portfolio, really. He was sure they all thought he had a laptop and other "manual" material. He calmed himself at the very thought of his novella in the recessed pocket with all of his personal writing. He suppressed a smile at the thought of writing his own story.

*Colonel Walter Kurtz*, he thought. *What would you think of this heart of darkness?*

He looked up to see the water again and wondered who arranged and did the work. It hinted to some degree of creativity, and it looked pretty. Two concepts that went against the well-established norms of consistency, productivity, and efficiency.

Marring the constructed natural sight were several banks of monitors with ongoing news that spilled over the flowers. While there was no sound but instead closed-captioning, the water could still be heard over the din of shoes and high heels clicking away. The lack of human voices talking no longer surprised him. He looked at a larger monitor and was struck by the vision of a large celestial body, a large planet, gracefully floating by. He slowed to a stop and approached the monitor. He was surprised by how clear and real-looking the image was before him. He was puzzled. To date, Central Corporate Command & Mainframe Control had always provided detailed animation and representation rather than actual satellite pictures. The decision to send satellites to meet and explore the rogue planet had been dismissed decades ago as a monumental waste of taxes, time, and productivity.

He stood and read the captions. He must have looked like a child staring at a new toy. He suddenly wondered if toys were still made. Finally, Gabriel saw why the satellite pictures looked real. They were, in fact, real transmissions. He did his best to suppress a smile and to look as disinterested as possible. He pulled his hand away from stroking the stubble on his chin. The unconscious behavior had already drawn the attention of his supervisor. "Not appropriate," she had stated in her disciplinary memorandum.

He looked closely at the massive size of the dark planet as closed captions scrolled by. After all the reports of how the lunar colonies had wasted resources, time, and money to simply witness and explore the event, new data about the rogue planet's actual trajectory, speed, and composition had come to light. The next images were of celebrating humans on the moon in their multicolored, different style clothing and a disarray of material all around their command and control center. The people looked pale, larger, but enthusiastically happy.

*Were they always this emotional? Happy? Were all of them celebrating?*

The image then shifted to more lunar citizens in larger areas all rejoicing wildly by Earth standards with public displays of affection such as kissing. But just as suddenly, many of the more official members looked surprised and gravely concerned. And that is when the live transmission ended and more information on power consumption came online.

*Wow.*

Gabriel pulled himself away from the monitors for fear that he would break down in joy, grief, or both. He was thrilled to see that such liberal expression of emotions was possible. But then *those* people were all on the moon or two miles under the Earth's crust. He tried to pick up his pace to get out of the building in case his actions had been noticed by either security or human resources. He clutched his portfolio as he moved quickly.

*I was born at the wrong time, wrong place.*

He walked straight to the building's doors with his head held down to avoid eye contact. Not that it mattered, with everyone watching their own programming on their computer wear. He had often fantasized about requesting to go to the moon or work in the Earth's crust. While getting to the moon would be a problem now that it was independent and its own sovereign world, becoming a "miner" in the underground nuclear power and thermal heating power plants would be far easier.

*All you have to do is cry. Laugh. Be happy…be human…I wonder why they all got serious all of sudden.*

A sudden surge of anger began to form in the pit of his stomach. He pushed the glass door with more force than he'd expected. He could feel the looks he was getting from those closest to him. In the sea of black, brown, and blue suits, he felt self-conscious. He would have continued in his dark thoughts except he saw a woman he knew. Slowing his pace, he quickly evaluated the situation. Surrounded by the building's security team and the human resources director, the petite woman in the gray suit looked ashen and tearful.

*Veronica? What?*

He slowed down more to listen in to what the emotionless human resources officer was saying.

"It is clear that you watched the rogue planet images and teared up. When I attempted to see you, you left the building," the officer said.

"It is time to go home," she said weakly.

"You are second shift, Ms. Sykes. You are not designated to leave your work area. Further, you demonstrated more emotional leakages this past week and avoided your sessions with Dr. Breitbart for treatment," the man continued.

"I-I forgot," Veronica started.

"Negative," a female officer said. "You were reminded one hour before today. When I came to find you, you had left your work area again. What is in your portfolio?"

Gabriel clutched his own bag. Then he realized that the security officer had told Veronica to open hers. His heart raced and his stomach felt like lead. Just like he and no one else, she, too, had a carrying bag.

*No! She probably has my book! She's going to get into so much trouble! No!*

Gabriel came to a full stop mere feet from the scene. The sea of changing shifts of dark suits continued to ebb and flow, leaving the drama to unfold. Gabriel felt a pang of sympathy. He had seen her several times over the course of the year. She would risk a short nod and even a suppressed smile whenever they would pass. Then the poetry on napkins where the other sat at break began. Beautiful poetry and then quotes. Once he reciprocated, it was as if a secret companion, a like-minded fellow, had joined him. And now she was going to be exposed.

*No. I can't lose her like this*, he thought.

As he stared, he saw another officer looking beyond his own computer glass wear watching the scene. Expressionless, the officer said something into his glass piece.

Compassion? Fear? Angry about hiding in the background, Gabriel felt his heart break for Veronica. Without further delay, he spoke as he approached the small group. A female officer at first moved to block his approach.

"Veronica? Are you telling on me? You're such a spy!"

Veronica's head snapped up, and looked at him. She did a poor job suppressing her surprise.

The female officer who'd first approached him came to a stop.

"What are you saying, Mr. Lawless?"

With little effort, he expressed himself with zeal.

*What am I waiting for? I won't sign that letter! I'll never wear a suit again. I hate you all!*

"What I'm saying is…is that woman has been spying on me! I can't stand it anymore!"

"Why is she spying on you, Mr. Lawless? Ms. Sykes was not enlisted to observe you nor have you reached surveillance level five," the human resources director said.

"She found my book and was going to bring it to security after I left!" he cried out.

His anger came in full force as he saw all the passersby stop to watch what must have been for them an emotional explosion in the midst of their tranquility.

*I hate you all…*

Gabriel pushed the female officer away and unzipped his briefcase and thrust his hand deep into the recesses to retrieve his own, worn written work and another old paperback book. Before he could even retract his hand, two sets of electrodes clipped onto his chest. Before the current from the electrodes even fired, he smiled.

"At last," he said.

A bright light flashed before him and he felt his muscles

lock up and then shake as the electricity ripped through his body. He felt only his nerve endings on fire, and then the ground rushed to his face. Darkness enveloped him. Still, he felt happy.

# AD 2140—En-route to Wyoming—Two Miles under Earth's Surface

*Join the company of lions rather than assume the lead among foxes.* —The Talmud

"So, how fast do you think we're going? Must be more than a hundred miles per hour," Gabriel said.

He didn't bother turning to hear what his companions might say. He was sure they would say nothing. Sitting in an eight-seat personal rail transport, he just couldn't contain himself. If not for the competency hearings and evaluations and finally judgment, he might have been heading in the other direction in his gray suit. He promised himself he would never wear a gray suit again. Based on his procreative competencies in producing two "productive and logical children" and a carefully constructed letter of support from his ex-wife, the court was willing to try two years of readjustment treatment and immersion therapy. But it didn't work out that way.

Instead, Gabriel Lawless was wearing a bright orange jumpsuit in shackles looking out of a speeding dark tunnel as he was whisked along to Deep Station Power Plant Six just outside of the old deserted state park once known as Yellowstone. Two point three miles deep in the planet's crust, he was on his way to join a small underground colony of miners—men and women castaways who either chose to join or were forced to join as a form of atonement, exile, and forced productivity. There were even rumors that the population had grown into a city. The station provided no reports, just power. The cities on the surface needed power, and the underground power plants around the world had provided them—nuclear and thermal for the last eighty-three years. While the nine worldwide underground stations did not declare their own independence like the lunar colonies, they behaved as such, remaining separate, silent and removed from their surface-dwelling cousins. There were even stories of the existence of dogs and cats, former pets that were eradicated on the surface due to their lack of efficiency and their tendency to inspire emotions.

Gabriel felt like an unbridled child again. Since his arrest for collecting and distributing books, especially fiction, and his lack of productivity, he had been processed as a criminal. When he awoke from his electroshock, it was as if he were a new man. As soon as he found out that Veronica had been cleared of possessing his novel—*A Tale of Two Cities*—he quietly rejoiced, and then punched his guards several times before he was subdued again. Such violent actions were not only unheard of in an ordered society, they were not tolerated. Treatments, isolation, and threats of punishment were all met with quotes, phrases, and words his captors could not understand. Still, through it all, he was always surprised to see that Dr. Samuel Breitbart, resident human specialist of Central Corporate Command & Mainframe Control for the Northeast Sector, was always there, always trying to help with his calm, soft voice, which approximated soothing better than any human or computer to date.

Seeing his own reflection in the darkness, the bright orange made Gabriel stand out from the six guards and Dr. Breitbart. A rounded, bearded face had replaced the thin one of last year. Up four sizes, he felt light on his feet even though he had surpassed his protein quota and body mass index as a result of constant lifting of heavy things to build muscle strength. He raised his shackled hands to stroke his graying beard. He liked it and smiled. He saw Dr. Breitbart looking at him curiously in the reflection.

"So, Sam? What's the look about?"

"You are like so many I have escorted to your final destination," he said calmly.

"Am I heading to a firing squad, doc?" Gabriel had come to like the stoic, calm doctor. Throughout all the trials and hearings, Dr. Breitbart had always been trying to help save him.

*A human trait, finally.*

"We do not use capital punishment. It was banned seventy years ago."

"Yeah, I know that, doc. My point is I'm heading to a place that no one has ever come back from. Nothing but audio communication. Weird but it might be interesting," Gabriel said. He was apprehensive. He had requested to go to the moon, but both Earth and lunar officials had declined due to not having enough castaways to economically send to the moon at this time. If they had, the lunar government would have granted the asylum.

Instead, he was heading to the underground power plant facilities. Built more than eighty years ago as a way to protect energy sources from the ravages of weather, they started out as small groupings shortly after the lunar secession. After years of operation, all the underground cities continued generating power but went silent for the most part.

"The colonies' rationale on limiting their visual contact is to maintain social order. Their citizens know nothing of what we have. If they did, they would leave their posts. It is a unique approach. They are obviously not as free as our society," the doctor said.

Gabriel felt his eyebrows rise. He turned to look at the doctor, who seemed engrossed in something that had come across his eyeglass screens. While the other guards stood around him and watched him carefully, Gabriel laughed out loud. It startled his watchers. It took him a moment longer to collect himself before he spoke. The shift from joviality to seriousness was natural to Gabriel now, but it had to be difficult for his logical, emotionless companions.

*A year of free expression will do that*, he thought. With the relative quiet of the cart flying on its rails, he found himself sighing before he spoke.

"You think you're free. You are not. It is an illusion, a mirage you cling to so you can feel safe and secure. I have lived your way for thirty-nine years and watched my life slip into gray. My children vanished into the corporate and industrial system to become logical, highly productive cogs of a mindless, dead, soulless society while the woman I once loved replaced me with a substitute. I would have done anything for my family. But to be gray in a world of dark suits, and black and white? No. Two miles in the Earth's crust with no contact with *your* kind? It is better to reign in hell than to serve in heaven," Gabriel said. He looked back into the speeding darkness, sure that they had all missed his literary reference.

*Milton, Dickens, Melville, Poe....I really miss my collections*, he thought. That was truly his only regret.

Two hours of silence transpired until he felt the large electromagnetic personal transport decelerate to a smooth stop. Gabriel took his time to look out the dark window and then all around the others to see if there was anything visible to see. He slowly stood up with his shackles in place and his guards moving in unison around him as he approached the door. The door hissed open and the smell of damp sulfur and heat was evident. He stepped out onto a dimly lit platform and followed Dr. Breitbart. He looked around until he finally noticed that all the guards had their computer glass wear off.

"Hey, doc, what's the deal with your electronics?"

"The tunnel's walls are at low levels of radioactivity even though they are lined with lead. No electromagnetic waves can penetrate without a direct corded line in or out."

"I guess that's another good way of keeping silent,"

Gabriel said more to himself than to the others.

"Yes," the doctor said. Gabriel was surprised at the level of discomfort he expressed.

"What's the matter, doc?"

Surprisingly the doctor answered quickly, as if his concerns were top of mind.

"The shielding against electromagnetic and carrier waves and all forms of wireless communications for the one route in and out of such a large complex, and the colonies' insistence on remaining isolated for years with near to no interaction with us above, has always...worried me," he said.

Gabriel looked at him a moment to consider the doctor's concern, something rarely seen in a citizen.

After a short three-minute walk down an empty metal ramp that reverberated with every step, they finally came to a large metal door. A very old case hung on the wall right beside the entrance. The doctor opened it and typed in a series of alphanumeric symbols. As soon as he retracted his hand, heavy mechanical latches and bars moved, opening the ancient door. Gabriel watched the old door move slowly and was impressed with its thickness, which had to be close to three feet.

"Is there anything you would like to record for the transcript before you enter?" Dr. Breitbart asked. As always, it was as close an approximation to kindness as he had ever heard.

Still listening to the loud gears, Gabriel spoke as he saw the door was opening only a little bit to allow one person to squeeze by.

"'It is a far, far better thing that I do, than I have ever done; it is a far, far better rest that I go to than I have ever known.'"

Dr. Breitbart nodded as if he understood. Gabriel felt the guards move him firmly through the door's narrow entrance. Their zeal in pushing him through quickly was a testament either of their desire to unload their charge or to escape the setting or more likely both. As soon as he cleared the other side, he heard the heavy doors gears again and watched what little light there was from the outside fade. For just a moment he wondered if it was a mistake to embrace feeling and push against the system. A quick recall of the laughter, the reading, and the total expression of life over the last year flashed before him as if to confirm that it was the right choice.

Finally the door closed solidly behind him and he stood alone, shackled in darkness. After a few seconds, a female voice came over an old-fashioned intercom. A sudden hiss of air came at him from all sides and an amber light slowly emerged from the walls.

"Well, well, well, Mr. Gabriel Lawless. Quoting Charles Dickens as you depart the world above? Impressive and contextually perfect. Now what is the rest? '"It was the best of times. It was the worst of times, it was the age of wisdom, it was the age of foolishness, it was the epoch of belief, it was the epoch of incredulity...' Welcome to your final destination."

As Gabriel struggled to raise his hands to protect his face from the pelting air, he was baffled and surprised at the voice's tone and that it had registered the Dickens reference.

*She knows Charles Dickens? How? Where am I? What is this all about?*

Gabriel could barely talk as the voice continued. Its tone shifted from amused to instructional, as if the person had shifted personas from professor to soldier.

"Once the forced air cleans your clothes of dust and dirt, please proceed to the door at the end of the corridor. There your shackles and clothes will be removed, and you will be cleaned, processed, and welcomed to your new home."

Still in shock, Gabriel did his best to follow directions. He was surprised at how the voice had sounded pleasant, and yet it seemed to express both humor and an undertone of darkness.

*Where am I?*

As promised, a series of machines came to life, his shackles and clothes were removed, and he was run through a series of multiple showers of many different liquids and vapors. His skin felt just a bit raw but cleaner than he had ever experienced. At the end of all of it, he found a warm, soft red towel and a clean tan jumpsuit and comfortable shoes. Confused but free of shackles and dead skin, he was also dressed, clean and focused on the large door in front of him. He stood there quietly and waited. As with the first door, the heavy mechanical hinges stirred and the door slowly opened. While the light in the cleaning area was a low, ambient illumination, the light on the other side appeared brighter. Gabriel was afraid. Afraid of what was next, not of death. As the light grew, his mind raced to what the voice had said earlier.

"'…it was the season of Darkness, it was the spring of hope…'" he muttered.

# AD 2142—Deep Station Power Plant Six, Wyoming—Two Miles under Earth's Surface

*Hold no man responsible for what he says in his grief.* —
The Talmud

"This is why we can't have nice things in the Welcome Center," a deep voice said.

Gabriel moaned at the voice, fully aware of who it was and where he'd most likely ended up. He forced his crusty eyes open but they were reluctant to comply. While his raging headache made itself known, his attempts to stir were rewarded with aches and pains. Lying on his side away from the voice and the seemingly bright lights, he managed to roll onto his back. Parched throat, headache settled in his forehead, and every bone in his body aching, he did his best to focus on what had happened in the last forty-eight hours.

"As always, lieutenant, Lawless lived up to his name," the deep voice said. It was without judgment but pointed out the irony of his name and the situation. Gabriel slowly moved his left hand to his left cheek. Without need of a mirror, he could tell by the swelling and the dull pain that his eye was sporting a pretty good shiner.

*Just great.*

"Come on, constable, this is the second time he's done this. And it's always pretty predictable; something happens on the surface and he's trying to get up there," a female voice said.

"He's been here for two years. He should know better."

"Can you blame him?"

"No, lieutenant, but we already got three new arrivals I have to watch. I don't need him giving my people combat lessons. And shouldn't he be a role model for his students? For a guy who got Teacher of the Year and who's a fiction writer, you'd think he'd be tamer," the constable complained.

"He is tame when he is focused on his students. But it's different for the newer arrivals," the female voice said.

Gabriel moaned again. He knew the voice and made the connection.

*Damn it. Lieutenant Julia Rose and Chief Constable Hector Mendez. Nice job, Lawless.*

"Now, you actually chose to sponsor this guy? Why do you always take on the literate dumb asses? Looking for challenges? Don't you think running the outer perimeter patrol is challenge enough?" the constable asked.

"No one's perfect, Hector," she said.

"It's a good thing his kids love him," Mendez replied.

At the mentioning of the kids, Gabriel sat up quickly. His head felt like it was going to explode, and his muscles screamed out in pain. Dizzy from his sudden movements, he leaned back against the wall for support and remained sitting in his bunk. Blurry vision finally cleared to reveal a very large pale man in a security uniform peering down at him. Beside him was a striking blonde in military uniform. Similar to the man, she, too, was pale but her form was feminine even in uniform. And while she stood a foot smaller than the constable with her hands behind her back, she exuded no less authority.

"Well, well, well...the prince returns. What is it, Mr. Lawless? 'Something is rotten in the state of Denmark?'" the lieutenant said.

It took Gabriel a few seconds to recall where the line was from. For a lieutenant in the DS6 Special Forces, Deep Station Power Plant Six's own military service, the lieutenant was both literate and had a wicked sense of humor to go along with her own brand of justice.

"You know, lieutenant, you got a line for everything. I'm guessing one of your parents was a teacher?" the constable asked.

"Both were professors. And they taught literature and history."

"The *real* history?"

"Yup. Before Central Corporate Command and the computer mainframe got rid of it all. I really do hate them," she said.

Gabriel tried to chuckle at the repartee but found it difficult to move, let alone speak or laugh. He focused on talking first. He took a moment to find the right words and syntax.

"Is it Monday…" he croaked out.

"Zero six hundred, my smelly, hungover mentee. You have at least two hours to get yourself together and get to class. And just so you know, all of your students petitioned on your behalf so you could avoid cleaning out human waste collectors. For me, I was going to have you spend a month cleaning the nature habitat in addition to human waste removal. It's a good thing you have friends, Mr. Lawless." Lieutenant Rose's voice was melodious. Very different in real life than it had seemed the first time he heard her over the intercom in the decontamination chamber for new arrivals.

"Well, at least he's not in the service. He would have been drummed out a year ago," the constable added.

"Or promoted. Once again, his efforts, however sloppy, did find a potential security breach," Rose said.

"You find a silver lining to every cloud, don't you, lieutenant?"

Gabriel carefully held his head up with one hand, and he placed another on the bunk to help push himself up. He stopped to get his wind and started again in just a moment. He smiled at the thought of his students' kindness and activism.

Suddenly, he felt a pang of sadness. Sharp memories of his two children when they were much younger flooded his thoughts.

"They're still up there," Gabriel muttered.

There was an uncomfortable silence in the room. The only noise to emerge was the sliding of the transparent barrier to release him.

"I'll get you coffee to go and some aspirin," the constable said in a far more gentle voice. After two years of knowing him, Gabriel had rarely heard the officer sound compassionate.

Gabriel's field of vision was filled with Rose's image in front of him. His left eye took in less. She remained quiet, as if waiting for him to talk. At least two minutes went by before he spoke again.

"How far did I get?" he finally asked.

"You got to the Welcome Center's post screening center. It took three security officers and two civilians to take you down. I had warned them to bring stun guns but they didn't believe me that there is such a thing as 'old man strength,'" she said.

"I'm only forty-one," Gabriel said.

"And the oldest security team member who took you down was twenty-five. For all of us over thirty, we salute you."

Gabriel nodded. He moved slowly to the edge of his bunk and pushed himself up slowly to stand. It was a precarious effort with the aching in his body, head, and heart all crashing down on him at the same time.

"Gabriel…I won't pretend to know what you're going through. With only a handful of new arrivals, those of us who were born here have no idea of what it would be like to lose all that you had aboveground, again."

Gabriel caught the subtlety. The first time he lost everything was when he was arrested and started his process toward exile. That was under his control. But this time around was too much. And in a drunken state, he'd been determined to get to the surface.

*What were you going to do, dumb ass? Freeze to death?*
Gabriel nodded at her kindness. She extended a hand for him to move out of the stark holding cell.

"Watch your step," she pointed out.

Moving slowly, he looked around the observation room and saw that the other four cells were dark and empty. He turned to see that the plant's visual alarms were still flashing at "yellow," but they were on mute.

"Here you go, Lawless," the constable said. He had two porcelain cups of a warm, black liquid that Gabriel had learned to love. He gratefully accepted the coffee, as did the lieutenant. The constable also gave him three aspirins, which he immediately took and gulped down with some of the warm coffee. Rose thanked the security chief and continued walking through the small office into the narrow hallway.

"I want my coffee cups back, you two," the constable yelled after them. Rose waved back to him without looking and sipped her coffee as she walked.

Gabriel kept pace but did his best to savor his coffee, walk, and not make any sudden movements unless he wanted his head to fall off. Unable to walk side by side due to the narrow space and the various security personnel, soldiers and civilians already on their way to work or home, he stayed behind her and listened. It was a very familiar pattern. She would lead and talk, and he would follow and listen.

"While you were passed out from your attempts to get to the surface, Earth Central Corporate Command & Mainframe Control finally made the announcement that the rumors that Earth escaped its orbit three days ago are true and that it was the rogue planet's unusual powerful gravity well and strong electromagnetic field that disrupted the orbit."

"Any reason why the planet's gravity well was exponentially greater than that of the sun? I mean, I'm not a science guy but it makes no sense that a planet twice as big as Jupiter could have a more powerful gravitational pull than the sun. And what did it do to our sun?"

"Tell me about it. I'm a soldier, not a scientist. They tell me, I nod as if I understand and then tell my team and they do the same," she said. She kept her pace up and sipped more of her coffee. Gabriel shook his head. It was all too big an idea to get his head around to comprehend. The lieutenant continued.

"Surprisingly, civil discord and riots were nonexistent upstairs. The surface population's overall response is to go to work late, sporadically, or not at all," the lieutenant said. The tone of surprise was easy to spot.

"Command did a real good job drugging nine billion people with pills, entertainment, and memos," Gabriel said. His anger was still hot even after two days of alcohol-induced unconsciousness.

"I know. The dimming sunlight, disrupted weather patterns, and drop in temperatures were getting hard to explain. The surface dwellers never considered that their government might be lying," she said.

"We could have told them," Gabriel said. He didn't hide his emotion too well. Rose's response was classic.

"And then what? 'Hello, surface dwellers. Your government is lying to you, so listen up—we can accommodate five thousand of your civilians out of your nine billion people. Oh? You don't want the help? Just keep pumping the energy to us? All right…'"

It was easy to see that Rose was angry, too. For a compact woman drinking coffee, she could go from zero to one hundred herself. He sometimes forgot there were fifteen thousand other humans in their complex who might have feelings about their cousins on the surface.

"Some could have made it," Gabriel said with less anger.

"Gabriel, when we offered the Central Corporate Command places for their children, they asked us to forget them and make room for their elite and officers. When we refused, they attempted to take our complex," Rose said. It was her turn to get angry.

"I know, Rose…I was there," he said.

"Now it will take us months to cut through the debris and rebuild the transport to the surface. Maybe a year or more. And why? Because we're expendable," she said.

Even though the halls were filled with people and some dogs and cats, he felt as if he were alone with her. Finally the hall walls transitioned from solid stone to transparent aluminum and steel, granting an impressive view from above of several acres of farms illuminated with artificial lights and heated with geothermal heating. Light filled all the corridors and gave the impression of a bright, cloudless morning. It was easy to see the other connecting, transparent tubes forming a lattice of hallways all filled with people and pets.

"By then, all life will be gone on the surface, Rose," Gabriel said.

He watched Rose slow her pace to stop and look at him.

"I know, Gabriel. It's not like we didn't try to help," she said.

Gabriel looked down rather than look into her eyes, which he would always do.

"I know. It's just that it's…"

"Unfair," Rose finished. "Of course it is. A hundred years ago when we first saw this planet coming, we started the underground programs. And when Central reversed its decision, since the chance of being struck was not probable, they converted this sanctuary into power plants two miles into the Earth's crust, a great venture to power the world above. I was born here, Gabriel. My parents were born here, too, and my three children are miners like us all. It's unfair that we were relegated here. It's just crazy that we'll survive and the majority above will not."

"None of them will live…any life. Only the ones that have prepared."

The light from the farming areas subsided as the transparency changed back to natural stone. The transition to actual rock was an indication he was near the residence center.

"What's happening with the lunar colonies?" he asked.

He took another gulp of his coffee. Between the movement, aspirin, and coffee, he was feeling a bit human again. Changing the subject helped.

"They're all right for now. In about five hundred years, they'll be on their own path," she said. She took another gulp of her drink.

"Oh no. Really?"

"Yup. Life imitating fiction, Mr. Lawless. Your novel last year seems prophetic. The rogue planet not only messed with our sun and the inner planets, but the moon's orbit will break from us in about five centuries. Not as sudden or dramatic as our departure but it's pretty fast in astronomical terms, I hear. They'll be on their own spacecraft. At least they have enough resources to last centuries. Who knows. Maybe this is God's way of allowing us to explore strange new worlds," Rose said with a chuckle.

"No," he said.

"That imagination of yours sure has a knack for accuracy."

Rose came to a sudden stop and turned to look right at him. She then took his empty cup and moved to retrace her steps back. Gabriel looked around and realized he was in front of the living quarters he shared with eight others.

Before continuing, she turned back to ask something.

"Hey, Gabriel? I had a chance to review the video of you battling with security…"

"Lieutenant, you have no idea how sorry I am for all of that," Gabriel started.

"No, Gabriel, I got that. I wanted to ask you about the numbers you kept yelling out," she clarified.

Gabriel squinted his eyes and furrowed his brow in the hopes that such efforts would help him remember. The whole event was a blur. It must have been obvious from his face that he was drawing a blank.

"It was something like 'forty-two, sixty-seven, zero-nine, seventy'."

The answer flooded his brain. He recited the numbers robotically as if they were engraved on his brain.

"Latitude 42.6677 and longitude 71.1225…it's a place I used to take my kids. It was sort of a fort or clubhouse we found years ago. It was pretty deep in the ground under an old building. It was built for radioactive fallout. Maybe they remembered. I just thought, maybe…" he started.

"Maybe your children went there?" she said.

Gabriel looked down to hide the tears forming in his eyes. "It's stupid, I know," he said.

"Hopeful, Gabriel, hopeful. Nothing wrong in being hopeful. That's what keeps us all going," the lieutenant said. She pivoted on her heels and headed back down the corridor, ostensibly to return the constable's coffee cups.

"Thank you, Rose. Sorry I've been a pain in the ass," he called back to her. She waved without even looking back. He returned the wave and then his hand went to his eye. It was hurting less, too. He was sure his students were going to give him hell for his actions.

*Natural consequence for being stupid. I guess I'll be the living example of being held accountable and accepting the consequences. That's a good lesson plan for adolescents,* Gabriel thought.

"Yeah, you are a pain. You got a visitor, by the way," Rose added. "She came in last week on the last transport from the surface before we blew all access to the surface. It took us some time to figure out who she was," Rose said.

Before he could ask, she was already out of view.

"The last transport from the surface? Wow. That is one lucky person. I guess he's staying with us," he mumbled.

Gabriel turned to his door, keyed in his access code, and pushed the slider open. He was only two feet into his living area when he heard a joyous cry and felt a woman jumping into his arms. Shocked by the enthusiasm and hug, he let the woman hug him tightly while she sobbed. With few options, he just rubbed her back until the weeping began to subside and her death-like grip lessened. After a few seconds, he was able to finally peel the woman away to identify who he was holding. He held her at arm's length and looked at her to make sure he was actually grasping who he thought he was holding.

"My God...it's been years..." he muttered.

He pulled her back into another hug, but it was he who squeezed and began to cry.

"Veronica...I'm so glad you're here," he said.

# Purgatory—Part Three

Deep Station Power Plant Six—AD 2137—Wyoming, Two
Miles under Earth's Surface

*Truth is heavy, therefore few care to carry it.* —The Talmud

Maria Henry was just on the verge of an orgasm when her
personal communicator vibrated incessantly. She let go for as
long as she could until the rising pressure and feeling of
excitation melted away. The movement under the sheets
slowed to a stop. Her lover of two years must have heard the
vibration as well and picked up on his lost opportunity to help
her release her stress. It had been a long fourteen-hour shift in
the power plant's control room overseeing thousands of
workers and an even larger number of citizens working to keep
the underground world viable with water, artificial light, air,
plants, and an entire biosphere for more than fifteen thousand
people. Without even a pause, she reached over in the dimly lit
room to her table and fumbled to turn on her communicator.

"It's Mark, isn't it? He has this thing about timing," her
lover chuckled.

Maria found she was devoid of humor and just wanted to
turn back time twenty minutes to turn off her device.

"If he wasn't so good at scheduling shifts and handling
exports, I'd fire him! I was so close," she said. She pulled
herself out of the bed and stood in the small room. She tapped

her device and the smiling bearded icon of Mark Dempsey, energy export chief, came on. She found the annoyingly small button to turn the communicator on and end the unremitting vibrating.

"No one likes you very much, Mark! You're up too early, stay at work too long, and you're too damn clearheaded in the morning. It's my day off and I'm not even halfway through my sleeping cycle and you call me? Did we have a meltdown in Silo Eight or are the surface dwellers demanding more power?"

In a rare display of seriousness, her jovial and remarkably positive chief was far more somber than she expected. She had a fear that maybe it really was a catastrophic event.

*Damage to the power plants? Biosphere?*

"I'm really sorry to bother you, boss, but I got a four-person personal transport car heading to Welcome Center Three."

"That's it," she said. She felt a silk robe falling on her shoulders to cover up her naked body. She flashed a smile and worked her arms into the sleeves as she juggled the device. The robe was a gift from her paramour last year and she just loved the material. Maria was positive that Mark had caught sight of her naked breasts and her maneuvering. It wasn't the first time her chief had.

"So you get me out of bed for an unexpected transport? Maybe it's one of the gray suits, the surface walkers, calling it quits upstairs to voluntarily join us. It happens. Once, I think," she said.

*Maybe twice in two decades.*

"Not this time, boss. We got a call from half a mile out asking us to 'receive three packages from Lazarus.' Any idea what that means? And how the hell did they manage communication while in transport? Their electronics and communication should have all been rendered useless."

Maria froze in place. The phrase was a code she never thought she would ever hear. Maybe from some other boss thousands of years from now or later, but not now. It took her a full minute to realize that she must have looked like she'd seen a ghost.

"Okay, boss, you're scaring the shit out of me. What's the deal?" Mark asked.

His voice pulled her back. An immediate plan of action came into place. It was a well thought out protocol and operations plan. Not since the lunar bases seceded from Earth decades ago had she thought she would be pulled into a life-or-death situation on a global scale. Maria moved as she spoke.

"Mark, I want you to clear the Welcome Center of all staff and have Security Chief Mendez meet me there in ten minutes. I'll brief you later. No discussion about this, and call in Alpha shift and keep Beta shift in place. I want all data and information on this matter locked down."

"Will do, boss" was all Mark said. She ended the call and already had her pants on when she gave up looking for her bra and put her work shirt on.

"Hey, Maria? Something big happening?" her lover, David, asked. He was still naked as she was moving to get fully clothed in mere seconds.

"Yeah. It's pretty big if I think it is what it is. I'll talk to you as soon as I know something," she said. She looked around for her left boot.

"It's under the chair, Maria. And I'll be back in about three days. I'm heading out to the outer perimeters to get heat and radiation readings," he said.

Maria's swift movements stopped entirely and she looked at him.

"Three days! Damn it!"

Her hands shot to her dark hair, through which she ran her fingers like a comb.

"I'm sorry, honey bee, but I'll be back as soon as I can to finish what I started," he said. At that moment he pulled her deep into an embrace and kissed her as if he were heading off to war. She felt light-headed and suddenly aroused. David's presence and touch had a way of pushing every frightening thing away.

"Damn," she said.

Maria would have held on longer but David's strong hands turned her around and pushed her toward the sliding door and slapped her butt as she moved.

"Three days, love," he said.

Once in the hall on the other side of her residential door, she moved slowly to allow her eyes to adapt to the slightly brighter light in the main corridors. Since it was in the middle of a sleeping cycle for Alpha shift, she was not surprised to see few people in the narrow walkways. As David's image and its wonderful aftereffects faded, she used the ten-minute walk to the Welcome Center to focus on the nuances of the Lazarus protocol.

*Hmm. Lazarus...raising someone from the dead. Usually something global and could be catastrophic. Three packages? Three people from the lunar colonies? Pretty damn risky for them to smuggle their way down here.*

"So boss? What's the deal?" asked Hector Mendez when he met her in the hall heading to the Welcome Center. "I was having a great dream about it raining when the chief called me."

Maria looked at him and was impressed that he was in full security uniform and not a hair out of place.

"What do you do? Sleep in your uniform?"

"The raining dream got me up to go to the bathroom so I was already on the move and down in the lavatory when the call came in," he said.

"And you always wear your uniform when you are outside your quarters?"

"Why, yes, boss. I'm chief of security. I'm always on," he said. Even as he spoke, his deep voice could not hide some of the sarcasm.

"All right, constable. Remind me to help you with recruitment of officers," she said.

"That would be much appreciated, boss. Nearly all my guys and gals are over forty-five. Smart and seasoned, but I need a whole lot of recruits and young ones to do some of the heavy lifting," he said.

With the exception of four other citizens, seven sleeping dogs, and three cats, they were pretty much the only ones conducting business. As they walked an additional ten minutes toward the receiving room, he gave her a status reports of the day's events, ongoing investigations, and upcoming events that would need additional overtime to make sure the areas were secure. He was just wrapping up his report when they were both in front of the main door from the Welcome Area to the receiving room. She keyed in her code and the heavy door opened smoothly all the way, letting them both into a smaller room attached to the personal transport ramp.

"You know, at some point, you might want to consider putting more barriers between the residential area and the Welcome Center and transport to the surface. It's likely that one of our smart-ass teens will try to take a joyride to the surface," the constable said.

"Noted," Maria replied.

*Who the hell would want to go up there? Work, sleep, produce, and stay chained to their technology? I don't know how they do it. My God, they're so boring.*

Her thoughts were interrupted by the sudden appearance and deceleration of a personal transport vehicle. In less than a minute, the transport's doors silently opened, and one man and two women emerged. While they were wearing the formal dark suits of the corporate surface dwellers above, their deliberate, economical movements, physiques, and eyes scanning the entire area spoke of something she had not seen for years except in old news reports.

"Now they're the most active military I ever saw. For moon dwellers in less gravity, these three look in pretty good shape," Mendez said. Maria nodded in agreement. She was about to smile and extend her hand to greet them when the lead man responded as if the prior comment had been meant for him to hear.

"We have been in covert operations in the field for the last five years, Security Chief Mendez," the male said. He extended his hand to Maria and shook it as he continued speaking. His grip was like a vise and she was glad when he released her.

"My name is Captain Maximilian Douglas, and my two team members are Lieutenant Roberta Lee and Sergeant Martha Owen. We are part of the Lunar Combined Military Force & Intelligence branch," the man said.

His voice was not as deep as the constable's but it was as firm as his grip.

"Well...nice to meet you. I guess you already know that I'm Maria Henry, plant boss?"

"Yes, ma'am. Nice to meet you," he said.

An unexpected silence fell over the scene. Maria found herself reeling from the flood of information and the invocation of the Lazarus protocol. Still standing in place, she decided to do what she always did when confronted by a series of events and data she was not happy with.

"Okay, captain. What do I call you?" she asked.

The two women behind the man stole a look at each other that spoke volumes. To the captain's credit, he smirked and visibly relaxed.

"You can call me Max. My mother had a thing for long names of German extraction. What can I call you?"

"You can call me 'boss' or 'Maria.' Never call me 'ma'am.' You can call Mendez 'constable,'" she said.

The man nodded. The two women behind him spoke up. They went by their last names—Lee and Owen.

"All right, no bullshit. Lazarus protocol, lunar military in plain view with the surface walkers, and part of intelligence no less giving it an added layer of pre-lunar secession—"

"We like to call it 'independence,'" Max said. Again, his military facade was gone and a more relaxed, amused person was standing before her.

"Well, they were successful, boss," Mendez said.

"Okay, independence, but this looks like the cold war years just before you guys bowed out and left the nest. Are you guys heading to Mars? Is that the plan? Was that satellite you allegedly sent to investigate our passing rogue planet really a cover to build an empire on Mars? Well, happy trails and good luck. Are we done here?" Maria asked. While it was part in jest, there was a tone of real seriousness to her questions.

"You have to admit it, Max. You lunar types are pretty secretive and only show up when shit is about to fall everywhere," Mendez chimed in. Maria liked it when the constable was around; they worked well together after two decades.

The military captain did very little in the way to deny the merits of the questions and did even less to obfuscate the matter at hand.

"Ten years ago, we discovered very unusual readings of the rogue planet heading our way. Its electromagnetic field was stronger than expected and its gravity was well beyond anything we would have imagined. Also, its size is too big to be a planet. It should be a star," he started.

"Is it still going to pass outside our solar system? There's no issue of collisions, is there?" Maria asked. The mere thought of a planetary collision that would damage Earth's crust and destroy the biosphere was too horrible a thought to consider. But Maria had plans in the vault for that, too.

"No, nothing like that at all. It's outside the solar system and well above the plane of Earth and the moon's orbit," he said. The soldier took a moment to organize his thoughts as if he was distracted by something.

"As you know" he continued, "we did send out two deep space probes to see what was going on with these anomalous readings. The first probe is sending back data that show absolutely insane gravitational strength from this thing. From what the science departments tell me, the gravitational strength there should have crushed the planet. It's nearly two and a half times greater than that of Jupiter and by all accounts should not exist in our universe. At the same time, we noticed that there are other time-space disturbances occurring in the wake of this rogue planet."

Maria felt as if her attention span was at full capacity. She was still trying to figure out what Max was saying when Lee jumped in.

"In other words, boss, this planet is linked to our time and space, but its physical science and laws of nature are operating on another plane of existence. It's like the whole planet is alien to our universe. It's something from another universe where the laws of science and physics are completely different from ours," she explained.

Maria was silent. Fortunately Mendez spoke next.

"So this rogue planet is from another universe? Not a really large planet from our universe?"

"In short, yes. It's like a physical sample of an entirely different kind of time, space, gravity, and electromagnetic waves that are floating through our universe. Hence the Lazarus protocol," Max said.

"That protocol is about disaster or a near-disaster event with a short window of time to prepare. How does this rogue planet affect us all if it's passing outside our solar system? It doesn't make sense," Maria said.

Max stepped closer to Maria and spoke in a low voice as if to calm her for what was to come.

"Even from outside of the solar system, this thing is pulling ultraviolet rays from our own sun. The gravitational pull from that planet is pretty powerful. It *could* disrupt Earth's orbit and might move it out of its habitual zone. It might even move all the planets out of their orbits. We just don't know for sure."

"Are…are you serious? *What?*"

Lee finally spoke. What she said was far from joyous.

"We have multiple simulations that suggest that the closer this thing gets, the more it will pull at our sun's corona."

Maria's eyes narrowed in confusion. Owen chimed in to fill in the gap.

"It's remotely possible that this planet's passing might increase solar flares and eject a significant amount of matter from the sun. Maybe enough to reduce both its mass and its radiance. The simulation keeps coming up at least a third of the time more frequently than all other projections."

"In that case, our orbit will move out along with all the other planets if the mass of the sun reduces, and it will get real cold if the sun's brilliance dims. It's a real bad day for us all as a species," Max said.

Maria kept looking into the soldier's eyes. They were a pale blue set and his hair was dark. She looked through them to see if she could see into his soul, to see if he was lying.

*Why the hell would he lie about something like this? It's too crazy.*

"We have data that we would like to share and get your ideas as to whether we are right or wrong or missed something," Owen said for Max. She produced a handful of computer chips and gave them to Mendez.

"No collisions but our orbit might be compromised," Maria said.

"Right now, we aren't seeing collisions in the future, but it's a moving theory. If it's *just* our orbits being disrupted, then the underground power plants and the lunar colonies become prime real estate for those on the planet's surface," Max said.

"Self-contained biospheres with unlimited energy, nuclear and thermal. Plenty of water and our own functional agriculture and food chain," Maria said.

"We'd be like a spaceship. The surface would freeze within years or months. I guess it would depend on how disrupted the orbits become. That would take a lot of mass loss," Mendez added.

Maria looked at the constable, surprised that the security chief was already speculating the end game based on different conditions. Her surprise must have been obvious.

"Basic physics, boss."

"Yeah, right."

"We're there already, but we have a lot fewer people on the moon than you do down here. There is one thing you people are missing," Max continued.

"What's that?" Maria asked.

"Security," Mendez said instead of Max.

Maria looked at him and wondered how he knew. Even as the constable spoke, it was easy to see that his mind was racing.

"We got three military specialists from the moon, not just your standard intelligence agents. That's all they do all day — think security. And these three have been above ground for years, probably assessing strengths and barriers firsthand. Now they're here and telling us this. I'm guessing they see us as possible allies and if necessary, a possible place to live in case the lunar colonies are compromised," he said.

Maria looked back at Max and the others. Both women nodded in agreement as Max spoke.

"If we are wrong, all the underground power plants will need to be fortified against any corporate takeover or sponsored military strike in the future. Maybe you'll even secede."

"You mean declare our independence," Maria corrected.

The man did smile. Maria's mind was now racing as she immediately assessed her resources and what needed to be done. She had been boss of the place for twenty-two years. It all came to her in the form of puzzle pieces.

*Is there time?*

"Yes, independence. That's if we're all wrong. But if we're right and Earth's orbit is compromised to an extinction-level event, the underground becomes a massive spaceship for the human species. While we are prepared, if something were to go wrong in our world, we need to have a plan B. As you can see, we have a vested interest in your survival to form this alliance," he finally said.

"And what about our corporate cousins on the surface?" Maria asked.

The empty reception area was quiet yet again for a long moment.

"I would tell them after we have helped you secure all entrances and exits to all nine power plants."

"How long do we have until this FUBAR happens? I want to clear my calendar," the constable asked.

"Five years we think before we feel it all, if anything. It should take us two to three years to prepare here and the others. By then, we will have a small fleet of transports for many of our people if the lunar colonies don't survive," Owen said.

"*Many* of your people?" Maria asked.

"We might have to make some hard decisions we would prefer never to have to make. If we experience a significant failure, thirty percent of our population, women, children, and scientists, will be on the first waves out. The children will be able to adapt to Earth's gravity more easily, we hope. The rest of us will remain," Max said. It was the first time Maria had seen the virile soldier appear sad and small at the same time.

"And we speculate that your capacity might be able to accommodate that number, but we'd have to see," Lee added.

"We're hoping, but we three have been planet-side for years. It took us a long time to get used to Earth's gravity," Owen added.

Maria looked down for a moment. In less than an hour, her entire role had changed from running an oversized power plant for her biosphere to overseeing an ark to preserve the species.

"Shit," she said.

"I second that, boss," Mendez said in agreement.

# AD 2142—Wyoming, Two Miles under Earth's Surface

*Examine the contents, not the bottle.* —The Talmud

"Are you sure we're going to be getting the transmission at the same time your people do?" Maria asked.

"We'll be getting it in less than ten minutes," Max said. He looked at Owen, who nodded to confirm.

The plant control center was busier than usual, and since it was always busy, it was far more chaotic, frenzied, and rushed as staff moved from one console to another, confirming figures and shouting out statuses and numbers. Maria stood in the middle of the large control room holding her own tablet and looking at her own bank of monitors. To her left, the energy and export chief, Mark Dempsey, was on his headset, talking to a number of different engineers and logistics specialists out in the field at the farthest reaches of the plant. To her right was the constable, talking to his own security team and the newly developed military team leader, Lieutenant Julia Rose, a woman who had to be in her late thirties. Once her security chief finished talking to his field officers and the lieutenant went off to her own separate bank of monitors, Maria nodded her head at him to ask him a question.

"Is it me or is she kind of old? I mean, I'm glad Max and his team helped put together our own little army, but I thought they were looking for the young ones. The other three officers are almost as old as she is. What's the deal?"

"We're looking for leadership qualities and experience to deal with volatile situations. She's a teacher," Mendez started.

"A teacher? She has experience in dealing with hostile situations and dangerous people? A teacher?" Maria asked.

"She taught high school for the last fifteen years. She's taught literature and history and had the highest success rate in student attendance and the students had the highest grades. And the guys who think they're hard assess came out from her class smart and reformed. She's a natural leader, boss."

It took Maria mere seconds to understand the connections. It was an understatement to say the miners were rowdy, smart, and opinionated with a healthy dose of raw emotions at the very surface. Add adolescents to the mix and it was as if all those qualities were on steroids.

"Makes sense to me," she said. "Now who's going to teach her youths now?"

"That was a big problem until a guy came in from the surface two years ago. Name is Gabriel Lawless," Mendez started.

"His name is *Lawless*? He had a name like that and lived up on the surface? No wonder they got rid of him."

"Their loss was our major gain. He's great with the kids. Rough around the edges. I'm surprised he didn't get here sooner, but that's me."

Maria nodded as she mulled over the new teacher's name. Mendez turned back to his headset and bank of monitors just as Owen and Lee came up to consult. Maria turned back at her own monitors and looked at the roster of those assigned to the perimeters, especially the two-mile-long rail system. Much to her chagrin, she was closely monitoring the project of setting charges along the tunnels in case all of civilization above them fell into chaos and Central Corporate Command decided to simply take over the underground plants for their own survival.

"Almost done," she said to herself.

She looked closely at the project and saw that the fire

teams were behind schedule but moving quickly. David had been clear that there were two ways to collapse a tunnel. One way was to rig it so that when it was blown, digging out would be next to impossible.

"That's easy," he had said. "But we'll never see the surface again and eventually lose air."

Much to her surprise, collapsing key sections and specific parts would be very effective in keeping out intruders for months and allow them to dig out, but it took a lot of time to calculate and implement.

*Very long process but good plan.*

She looked at the roster and saw that David's name was not on the lead team today.

*Thank God!*

Maria's mind wandered to how the other power plants were doing with their preparations. Since the lunar team came to them and broke the news, she and Power Plant Six had become the unofficial leaders of the entire underground movement. Her world had also received an unprecedented increase in population from the agricultural and ocean sectors. Upon hearing the news from their underground cousin, the farming and fishing leaders had decided to transition all their youths under twelve years old and women under thirty-two who wanted to leave. Her small city of fifteen thousand miners had now grown to twenty-five thousand.

Surprisingly, the five-year transition had gone smoothly, especially with the additional skills and resources the new miners brought with them.

*I wish we could have worked with the corporate command like the others. Just great.*

"Transmission is coming in. If all goes well, we'll have a split screen. One with our lunar command and the other a direct feed to what the probe is seeing," Max explained.

The control room dimmed just a bit as the large floor-to-ceiling screen came to life.

"Lee? Mendez? Make sure you send what we got directly

to the Mainframe Control upstairs. Maybe they'll run it," Maria said.

"If it's good news for them, they will," Owen commented.

The left side of the screen showed very serious-looking lunar scientists strapped to their seats so as to keep from floating.

*Now why do they need straps if they're sitting still?*

Suddenly, there was a burst of cheers and shouts of glee. Their sudden motion explained the wisdom of the safety belts. Others in the back of the view hugged and kissed each other, and as a result were floating in the direction of the greatest force.

The right side captured a star field only.

"Where's the planet?" Dempsey asked.

Maria was wondering the same thing, too, until she realized that near the center of the screen was a sphere of blackness as if there were a black, solid object blocking out the stars behind it. As the camera angle focused on the lower part of the view, the sun's reflection dimly illuminated the leading edge of the planet.

"Is our sun reflecting on the bottom part of the rogue?" Owen asked.

No one answered in the control room, but a series of data, diagrams, and computer-generated images outlined that the massive rogue planet was well above the orbits of all the planets and the sun.

"Well, that's good news," Max said aloud.

The lunar control room which had been loud and noisy five minutes earlier was now deadly silent except for sounds from clicking computers, recycling air, and people exhaling. As Maria and her team listened in on the lunar scientists' communication, the images and animated models were flashing different scenarios based on the new data and their projections. After a minute of flashing, a fresh computer-generated trajectory and filters projected the rogue planet's course and effect.

Maria watched intently. Time passed. How much time? She had no idea.

The image showed the dark planet speeding up as it approached the sun. In addition to its massive size, the rogue planet's speed was unnaturally fast. Its course put it well above and beyond the solar system plane, but its passing was about one point six astronomical units directly above the sun, or a bit farther than Mars's orbit. While that was a relief, as the planet came closer and its illumination grew, the sun's coronal mass ejections increased in both frequency and intensity as the proximity increased. As the sun's filaments grew still longer and became more violent, the ejection of plasma and mass was impressive. Only the computers could assess and compute the mass being ejected. Maria knew there was energy well above and below the range of visible light. More time passed. Her shirt was nearly soaked through with sweat just like everyone else's.

"Holy shit," Dempsey said. "The sun's mass…the sun is blowing out its mass! Look where it's going!"

Maria looked at her monitors and back up to the larger one. On the left side, the scientists' joy and enthusiasm had long vanished and had been replaced with determined brows and ashen expressions.

"Dempsey! Cut to full screen on the right side," Maria said.

The split screen continued and didn't change. She looked back at her energy and export chief and saw that he was frozen like everyone else, staring at the images that were playing out.

"Mark? Enlarge the right side," Maria said again. She watched him shake out of his trance and moved his hands to comply. The serious-looking lunar scientists and personnel vanished and the computer simulation enlarged.

As their own sun dimmed, the rogue planet's illumination was blinding. Then, without warning, the rogue planet flickered and winked out of existence, as if it were never there.

Maria looked at the empty screen and blinked her eyes

many times. She looked around the room to see if she was the only one looking for the rogue planet that had illuminated instantaneously to the level of the sun and then just disappeared.

"Did it blow up or something?" someone asked from belowdecks.

"It's like it reached critical mass, or something," Maria said aloud.

"Chief? Roll back the time index to before the rogue starts flickering and focus on the inner planets," Mendez said. Maria was still grappling with the entire scene, but she did notice something in the constable's voice. It was something she'd never heard from him.

*Fear? From him?*

The angle changed and the images went backward to the point requested. As it went forward once again, a series of calculations and numbers flickered beside Mercury, Venus, Earth, and Mars. After a brief scan, it was clear that as the mass of the sun decreased significantly. The loss of mass was at a rate not possible based on the numbers. A series of monitors was running and repeating the computations and projections. The silence of the room was deafening. More time passed. More silence interrupted only by clicking, breathing, and air circulating.

"Talk to me, people," Maria said eventually.

"Rebooting mainframe and backup for confirmation on data," a female voice said.

"Pulling up most likely simulation on the main screen," the chief added.

"Lunar command is running its own series of numbers and it's looking grim. Owen—check my numbers," Max said.

"I keep coming up with the same data and simulations: the sun's gravity has weakened. This is allowing the orbits of the planets to expand outward," Lee said aloud.

There was more silence, as if Lee had pronounced their death sentence.

*We are so screwed…*

"Speed up the simulation of the planets' orbits and put them on the main screen, full size," Maria instructed.

She already knew the answer. As the time indexes sped up while months passed rapidly into years, the chief stopped the time at the seven-year mark, AD 2149. By then, the orbits of all the planets were profoundly different and the entire solar system was changed. The Earth was still outside the asteroid belt but was beyond Mars's original orbit. Mars was ablaze with impact craters and volcanic activity as stray comets and asteroids were caught in its gravity well from entering the retreating asteroid field, while Neptune and Uranus were no longer held in orbit at all. As the orbits shifted, the sun's ejections of plasma had continued to accelerate, showing no sign of slowing.

"Earth's orbit at this point is about seven hundred twenty-four point ninety-five days," another voice from belowdecks said.

"We're going to need a whole new set of calendars," Mendez commented.

"The sun is still losing a massive amount of mass," Max said.

"It's like that rogue planet started a chain reaction or something," Owen commented.

"That thing accelerated our sun's life to a red dwarf," the chief said. His tone was that of resignation.

"And disappeared. How the hell does that happen? A planet that size?" Lee asked. Hearing her voice again reminded Maria that the plan to move their defensive perimeters was no longer critical.

The time index sped up to AD 2200. The chief stopped it there because the computer-generated simulation looked very different. He dialed it back to replay several more times before Maria spoke.

The planets Earth, Venus, and Mercury joined the rest of the solar system as they reached their orbital escape velocity and were hurtling into deep space. The sun had dimmed to a much smaller, pale red sphere. The newly formed red dwarf star that replaced the powerful, younger solar system sun had no mass to hold the planets in place.

"This scenario should happen over billions of years and it will all happen in decades. What the hell…" the chief added.

"All right. The very thing we feared would happen, happened. That means we accelerate all defensive perimeters and secure all life support. We do this right, we live underground and the lunar colony goes on as usual," Maria said. As much as she wanted to crawl into a corner with David and sleep, she needed to keep her team going, focused and positive.

"People…we knew this would happen," she said again.

"Except about the disappearing rogue planet," Max said.

While Maria wasn't a scientist, her position of power plant boss meant she knew a lot about physics, numbers, and the role of mass and gravity. She decided to appeal to everyone's desire to figure things out to shake them out of their trance.

"How the hell does a rogue planet alter our sun's progression so that it goes from our sun to a red dwarf in hours?" she asked.

"It may have been depleting our sun for years prior at a different wavelength," Owen offered.

"And the sun continued ejecting mass after the planet disappeared," Lee added.

No other answers came for a long minute until Max spoke again. Maria started thinking of another strategy.

"I guess, boss, the scientists were right. That thing is not just a rogue planet. It's from another universe or plane of existence. I guess shit like that can happen when you're talking alternative universes and altered existence with other laws of physics."

With more than forty people in the control room, it was still quiet. The notion of the silent people triggered a thought.

"Mendez? Did all of this play up on the surface? Do the regular people know?" she asked.

Her chief of security needed to look over his monitors to figure it out.

"They cut it off before all the data were obtained. Looks like central corporate control is keeping its citizens in the dark," Mendez said.

"Shit. You know what that means, people?" Maria said.

"Our home just became prize real estate like all the other power plants underground," Mendez said.

"All of a sudden, the lunar colonies' self-contained and safe world looks pretty good," Max added.

"We got to move, people," Maria said to forty people. In mere seconds, the activity went from zero to ninety. Orders, data, and confirming information filled the air with a profound sense of urgency as people mobilized to keep their home safe.

Maria nodded in approval. She was glad that her people could get beyond the horrors of the future and focus on preserving themselves. She felt a rush of anxiety, however, but it was not about the Earth or even herself.

*Where are you, David?*

# AD 2142 (Four Days Post-Event)—Wyoming, Two Miles under Earth's Surface

*Sorrow for those who disappear never to be found.* —The Talmud

"Not now," Maria whispered. Her residential door's chimes had been ringing every fifteen minutes for the last hour. While she had secluded herself in her quarters for only three hours, she saw everything that was happening to her power plant via her monitors and tablets. When needed, she even jumped in to answer questions and provide leadership. Presently, she was still in bed, fully dressed and surrounded by a series of tablets as if she were in a nest. While the warning lights flashed yellow silently, indicating that the station was to remain at a hypervigilant status, the actual threat had passed days ago. The rogue planet had passed well above the solar system, depleted their sun of mass and plasma, converting it from a strong yellow sun to a weak red dwarf star, and then the rogue planet vanished through some kind of wormhole. Immediately after, the Earth along with all the other planets rapidly expanded orbit away from the sun due to the sun's loss of mass. At least that was how she understood it. And while that was on a grand scale of events, it was the mundane that crushed her. She sifted through her tablets and found the roster of the nine dead miners who'd set off the tunnel mines to keep Central Corporate Command's military from using them to gain entrance and seize her power plant, to take her world for their elite and military.

*They had no problem with the idea of letting us and everyone else die.*

"Why, David," she said quietly. "You knew I wouldn't do it, didn't you? You knew I wouldn't push the button if you and the others were still out there."

Her eyes were depleted of tears as she had cried them all in the first two days while still at her post. Her mind drifted to the minutes that followed her lover's death, when she realized he'd made the decision to save her and his home instead of letting her do it. And after that, Central Corporate Command had well articulated its threats and demands that she and all other power plant bosses were to be relieved of their posts and to expect "replacement personnel in three hours." When she and the other bosses went radio silent, the orders to walk away shifted to "comply or suffer catastrophic consequences."

*They've already taken my love, my life away,* she had thought.

Finally, when Command threatened to use biological weapons of mass destruction on her underground world, she made a decision to shorten Earth's life on the surface from years to months; she cut off all power to them. Military, offices, hospitals, anything in need of electricity was turned off in the entire eastern part of the continent known as North America. When the other power plants saw what she'd done, they followed suit without hesitation. Tunnels collapsed, power to surface dwellers was shut down, and her love forever gone, she now lay down in her bed alone. She mulled over everything that had happened and realized that David was right. If he hadn't done what he did, she might not have made the decisions that followed. In her state of mind as it was now, she would kill the world for losing David. Well, she had, at least those on the surface.

Her door chimed again.

"Go away," she said.

Instead, her locked residence door opened as if it were unlocked with an override code. She knew who it was even before his dark image appeared at her bedroom doorway. Chief Constable Mendez did not apologize for the intrusion or explain why he was there. He just stood quietly and waited for her to talk. In another state of mind, she was sure she would have thrown a fit, but she was not herself. Minutes passed until she spoke.

"I hate them all, constable. If it wasn't for them, David would be alive. If they weren't such emotionless automatons, we could have saved their children. But they wanted everything. They wanted our world so their elite heartless bastards could live here at the expense of us and everyone else," she said. Her tone and presentation were void of all emotions except sadness.

Mendez nodded. For a security chief, he was a good reader of character and listened well. He let the silence sit for a moment. She watched the large man shifting from one foot to the next, looking down at his feet as he often did when he was listening intently.

"I can't tell you it's going to get better or if you'll ever heal, boss. Only time and God can do that," he said quietly.

"Yeah," she muttered.

"But I can say this," he added quickly.

Maria could still feel her heart pick up at the thought of getting an answer for something she could not fathom to ever understand.

"Boss? What would David want you to do right now?" Mendez asked.

Maria found herself looking at her security chief. She wanted to leap across the room and strike him. Her heart raced and her breath came up short. But after just a second, she actually heard what the constable had said.

*What would David want me to do?*

She sighed and felt her heart settle back down. She released her balled fists and relaxed her entire body. After a minute more, she moved her array of tablets from the bed so she could get up. As soon as her feet touched the ground, she stood and looked right at him.

"He'd be pissed that I was not doing my job and would say something stupid, like most men would," she said.

Mendez nodded and looked back down at his feet again.

"We're pretty good at saying stupid things, boss."

She was just pulling up a couple of choice words and colorful metaphors for how the constable had manipulated her emotions to get her going, when her quarter's intercom came alive.

"Sorry to bother you, boss, but is the constable there?" Lieutenant Julia Rose asked.

Maria could see that her friend's shoulders physically slumped before he spoke.

"Here, lieutenant," he said.

"Just so you know, our 'Teacher of the Year' just left the tavern three sheets to the wind, and was heard saying he planned to get to the surface 'no matter what.' I'm heading Welcome Center Three and there's already a group of security en route. Problem is, they don't have any stun guns," she said.

"The guy's in his forties, right? My team stationed there is trained and far younger," Mendez explained.

"Ah, all right. But I wouldn't count on him going down easy. He's a father bear searching for his cubs and won't go gentle into that good night," the lieutenant said.

Maria wondered about her choice of words. Her puzzled expression caught Mendez's attention.

"All right, lieutenant. I'll meet you at the center and maybe you can talk him down. And don't use any of that literature stuff. It confuses us all," he said.

"No promises. See you in ten," she said.

Maria looked at him and could see he was not happy.

"It's Lawless, isn't it?" she said.

"Sure is," he answered.

Maria had met the newcomer once and liked him

immediately. For a former surface dweller, he had a lot of attitude and spunk. He was also courageous. There would have been thirty dead if it weren't for him and some of the older students who'd pulled some of the miners from the rubble from the collapsed tunnels.

The constable remained in place. She nodded and stood up on her aching feet.

"All right, constable. I got your point and will rip you a new one later," she said.

"No problem, boss. You heading to the control room?"

"Yup. That's what David would have wanted me to do," she said.

Without a further word, she walked out of her bedroom and quarters into a very crowded common hallway with Mendez right behind her.

"You deal with Lawless and I'll check in with the chief and Delta shift. Let me know what happens," she said.

The constable turned left as she continued straight to the control center.

"Will do, boss."

She walked in silence, though her once relatively empty common ways were filled with multiple personnel, dogs, and cats.

"I know, David. I'm going to work," she said quietly to herself.

# Hell—Part Four

Rogue Planet—Infinity—Alien Biosphere

*The sun will set without thy assistance.* —The Talmud

*"Cartographer, rise,"* the voices ordered.

Consciousness emerged for the first time in millennia.

*"Am I the last to awake?"*

*"Yes. All the others have been engaged."*

*"Have we arrived?"* the Cartographer asked.

*"Yes, Cartographer. What will the heading be?"*

The Cartographer shifted its consciousness toward the igneous crust of their planet facing the strong yellow star. The warm rays of the alien young sun of the small solar system were perfect. Passing right over it, the Cartographer assessed that the energy levels in the quartz strata were rising after billions of years of depletion, the time when they entered this strange, alien universe. While the sun's energy had been feeding their home for years prior at multiple wavelengths, the proximity would be just what was needed for terminal velocity. The carbon deposits awaited the planet's mantel spin to reach launch velocity, and the iron's electromagnetic field was near full capacity. All the other minerals, rocks and strata were primed to escape this infernal place.

*"I will not miss this universe,"* the voices said.

*"Why?"*

The Cartographer knew why but wanted to hear other voices. He appreciated the rest and the escape from the alien universe's void, but there was time before propulsion reached critical mass to bend time and space, and the absence of the voices was missed.

*"I will not miss its silence."*

*"Yes. Surrounded by those of our own kind—silicate, mica, quartz, feldspar, iron, diamond—all around us and yet they remain trapped to themselves, silent, devoid of sapience. How is this possible? This is a place of no hope,"* the Cartographer answered.

*"Nitrogen, oxygen, hydrogen, carbon-based life and light waves that act as both particle and waves are all very disturbing,"* the voices added.

*"Still, we will only be able to reach the halfway mark if all goes well. It will always be to the halfway mark. Forever."*

*"Yes. But maybe there will be others. Maybe more of our kind. Something to end the loneliness,"* the voices countered.

*"Yes. At least that."*

The Cartographer was nearly done with the required measurements and location to open a portal to finally escape this hell. The igneous crust was reaching a critical level and the diamond engines were near launch. The yellow sun's mass and energy were perfect. The planet's molten core sped up the iron mantle's photon buildup and the electromagnetic field expanded exponentially to provide shielding for transport.

*"Are you sure there is no life of our kind on these other terrestrial planets?"* the Cartographer asked.

*"No. They are all like the others in this place. Silence. Water. Elements. Carbon. No life as we understand it. Void. Emptiness. We long to escape this hell,"* the voices said in unison and pathos.

The Cartographer felt through the crust near the quartz beds and the igneous surface that all mass and energy extracted from the yellow sun were now at a perfect level. The mantle was at nominal levels, propulsion was initiated and the shielding was fully charged from the iron core. The internal mantle rotated faster, allowing the electromagnetic field to multiply in strength. More carbon beds were pressurized to form diamonds in case of engine failure. The emitting energy would increase their velocity to leave the barren universe.

*"We are ready, Cartographer."*

*"Yes. I will not miss this place. Do you think the next universe will at least have sapience of our kind?"*

*"We will see."*

*"Yes."*

The heat and vibrations of the planet's surface erupted outward and focused on one specific spot of space just ahead of its position. The fabric of time and space thinned at first and then expanded in brilliant light. After mere seconds, the barrier between universes opened and a conduit to another universe with its own natural laws, intelligence, and life awaited their arrival. As the rogue planet flashed and launched deeper into the corridor between universes, the voices spoke again.

*"I hear voices on the other side, Cartographer. Similar to our own…"*

After taking billions of years to travel, the Cartographer held the course and waited.

*"Finally."*

# Limbo—Part Five

Earth—AD 2145—Ruins of Merrimack College, Twenty-five Miles from Boston, Massachusetts

*Make your books your companions.* —The Talmud

"Marsha? Marvin? What are you doing out here? It is very cold," Rebekah Lawless said.

Marvin turned to see his mother struggling to get up the small rise to meet them on the empty, ancient road. While devoid of obstacles such as wheeled, tractor, and rail vehicles, it was the recently fallen snow over the permafrost and the protective multilayers of clothes she wore that were making it difficult for her to get traction and leverage. He moved toward her and pulled her up, since his footing was better placed in frozen footprints from that same morning. As he pulled her up, he looked behind her to make sure that the hatch to their old clubhouse was closed. She was right, however. Even in his multiple layers and covered face, it was remarkably cold. The sun's rays were diffused by the near constant cloud cover, giving it a more pinkish hue instead of its new red color. It was about one-third the size it had been just a few years ago.

"June 21, 2145, and the sun is as bright as a street lamp in dense fog," he heard Marsha say.

Marvin felt the corners of his mouth curl up at her use of images rather than her old efficient vernacular.

*She's been reading stories again.*

"Why would you use those images when simply stating that the sun's illumination is a third the strength and the fog is obscuring its limited radiance and warmth?" he heard his mother say.

*Poor thing. She can't give it up.*

With his mother and sister beside him, Marvin returned to looking at Boston's dark, frozen skyline in the early afternoon on the summer solstice. The once thriving metropolis was motionless and empty. None of the telltale signs of life was visible, no aircraft, rail traffic, or movement of any kind. With the lowest tier of the food chain knocked out, all vegetation, insects, animals, and humans were either dead or dying on the frozen planet. Surrounded by frozen, bare trees, his small family unit was the only visible life overlooking the empty vast plain toward the city. It was strange to see nothing in the sky. No drones. No aircraft. No sounds or light.

In the silence of early afternoon, Marvin imagined that in the old days when Earth was closer to its sun, the silence and stillness of the city might have been something experienced in the early morning at the break of dawn. Even then, there would be drones, rail traffic and aircraft. He remembered standing near the same place with his father and Marsha more than a decade earlier. There was nothing but life—the movement above and around Boston could be easily seen once the overgrown fields were cleared of vegetation, small animals, and so many bugs and birds.

*It was so warm then.Look at this place*, he thought. The vista always made him sad.

"So with a total of fifteen hours of sunlight scheduled for today, it's pretty close to freezing, I bet," Marsha said parenthetically. At every intake and exhale of precious air, the freezing vapors punctuated the fact that the atmosphere was very cold. And while breathing in the frigid air did not sting as much during the day, it was in the outside, nighttime air that breathing hurt more than exposure to the cold air that was well below zero.

"Yup. Not exactly the dog days of summer," Marvin added.

The family continued looking at the dark city's outlines until another cloud bank began to move in from the east. It was easy to see that dark, heavy clouds were also moving toward their barren, silent real estate. Marvin heard his mother speak in a rare moment of reflection. Her voice in the past several months had been weaker than usual, as if she were tired.

"It would have been logical to stay in the sanctioned safe zones in Maine," she said.

A flash of anger came over Marvin. He focused on watching his emotions so he could talk to his mother in a tone that she would understand. Strong emotions didn't work with most people. *That is when there were people.*

Marvin collected his thoughts before he spoke in an even tone that was forced.

"So that our *stepfather* could monitor our deaths from the comfort of his safe haven? Where he could be sure that we perished? I wouldn't give him the satisfaction." Marvin took a deep breath of the frigid air. It was very difficult to contain raw emotions now. With most of the people gone, it didn't matter so much. *Nine billion to maybe twelve million and dropping. God…*

"Screw him!" Marsha added.

"He might have been able to suggest that another, less efficient and less valuable personnel be sent out and we take their place," Rebekah said weakly.

"He had that chance for two months, Mother! And he did nothing. He wasn't going to do anything for us," Marsha said.

Her harsh tone took Marvin by surprise. But Marvin nodded in approval. Marsha had long resisted Marvin's plan to escape to the old ruins where his father and they used to explore. It was fun back when they were nine and seven. But when it became clear that their time on the Earth's surface was limited and that only the "multifaceted, efficient and gifted" would be taken into Central Corporate Command's arks,

Marvin watched his sister's steadfast loyalty to her stepfather wane and collapse when he alone was chosen to leave. In less than thirty minutes, his stepfather had packed some belongings and left his family behind.

*He didn't even take any pictures.*

If Marvin's mother hadn't insisted on following his stepfather's trail and waiting for him to rethink and take them in, they would have had three additional months to stockpile their own ark. While Marvin had started years prior, he still lost valuable time.

*That's time we'll never get back.*

"He cost us," he said bitterly. He couldn't keep the emotion out of his voice at the lost time.

Marvin was sure his mother was going to offer some response but was interrupted by a very young voice.

"Hey! Come on back in here! It's freezing," a seven-year-old voice yelled out. Marvin pushed away his angry thoughts about his stepfather's abandonment and focused on important things. He turned to see a little boy waving to him to come back in. The young boy was one of five children, ranging from seven to thirteen, whom they'd picked up along the way. While billions were dead and more dying every day and in the bitter cold night, there were orphans who chose to search for help rather than to passively wait for death.

Marvin waved back and turned to help his mother and sister down the small embankment. By the time they were halfway to the ancient basement metal door in the old abandoned Engineering wing of a university, a sudden squall of snow burst above them. He was thankful Jim had called them back. While they had only a short distance to travel, the snowstorm's sudden blinding appearance was commonplace on their cold planet. When it wasn't snowing small, dry crystals or when there was a break in the heavy, frozen clouds, the stars were so close and it made them feel as if they were the last people in a dark and empty world.

*Maybe we are now. At least on the surface*, he thought.

The irony was not lost on him how those relegated to the power plant cities underground or the independent moon colony were safe, warm, and probably prepared, while the reasonable, efficient, and productive citizens on the surface were all dead or doomed.

*Stop it, Marvin! That negativity doesn't help!*

"It's crazy how fast the storms hit now," Marsha shouted out over the howling wind.

"And the snow doesn't even make good snowballs," Marvin said in an attempt at humor.

"Not sticky enough," Marsha said.

"Well, that is because the lack of moisture at lower levels and colder air patterns at the surface keep the liquid to a minimum. With no surplus of moisture in the air, the snow cannot collect to form a snowball," their mother said.

Marvin closed his eyes and kept his mouth shut.

"That was humor, Mother," Marsha finally said.

After a very short trek and carefully navigating the stairs six feet belowground, Marvin closed the first of four heavy metal doors leading to the old fallout shelter that had been converted into engineering labs. Their footsteps echoed in the recesses of the old, dark, and deep ruins as their two flashlight beams cut through the darkness. Three doors and three barricading systems later, four more feet farther below the surface, they were at the final door that was held open by an eleven-year-old girl, Debby, who was smiling. She had an open can of multicolored food in syrup called "Fruit Cup." Marvin was happy to see her immediately offer some to Jim, who accepted with zeal.

"Best meal I've had in a week," the cute redhead girl said.

"Wow! Hey, I've saved mine from yesterday. Maybe it's the same kind," Jim said enthusiastically.

Both preteens ran off into a large main room. In the low light, Marvin took off his layers and shook off the snow that held on in the balmy fifty-six-degree work area. Marvin helped his mother take off her layers and then took their clothes to where they kept the other clothing gear and sleeping blankets.

"It is a shame," Rebekah said.

In a moment of hope and curiosity, Marvin waited for her to continue. Marsha was less patient.

"What do you mean now, Mother?"

While it was easy to hear the enmity in his sister's voice toward their mother, he was sure that she'd missed the entire emotional message.

"With our finite resources and eight people, our time alive is shortened," Rebekah said.

Though it was relatively quiet inside the large complex of rooms, the sounds of laughter, giggling, and talking were easily discernible. When compared to the tomb outside their constructed cave, their home was bustling with life and hope. Marvin readily sensed the coming emotional onslaught from his sister.

"So we should have left those kids to die out there? We should have done the logical and reasonable thing your husband did? You know, extend our resources and our lives together at the expense of five children? Is that what you're saying?"

"Marsha...let it go. She doesn't get it," Marvin said in a low tone. He motioned his hands downward and then pointed at the playing children.

Even in the dim room, he could see his sister's anger and his mother's expressionless reaction.

"I hate this," Marsha said. She stormed off toward the youth ostensibly to put distance between herself and her mother.

"I do not understand your sister," Rebekah started to say before Marvin cut her off with the raising of his hand.

He sighed and focused on controlling his anger so he could convey his message without emotions, in the hope that his mother would understand and comply. While only nineteen years old, he felt much older.

"I stopped Marsha's tirade so she would not upset the

children and their play. It was not to support your thinking. Do not say those things about resources, time, and what we should or should not have done. It's passed. There's nothing to be done about it, and reiterating the obvious is not helpful and will only provoke anger and frighten the children. Is that reasonable?"

He waited for his mother to respond. It came surprisingly quick.

"Yes," she said. Nothing else followed.

*Finally.*

Marvin looked around the dark room with its four battery-operated lamps shining in the dark. He moved away from his mother's side, took out his flashlight, and moved to another smaller room. He opened its door, stood at the entrance, and looked at just a few boxes, a mere fraction of what was stored three years ago. What had been a mountain of boxes filled with an assortment of canned water and food, old freeze-dried survival rations, and military field rations was down to just a few large boxes. Everything that was there had been gathered over the course of the five years either online or by physical purchase. All done before the flood of orders took everything. Next he had scoured the old buildings outside Boston before the road vehicles and rails were seized. While weapons were not accessible, blankets, cots, clothes, and other necessities had been carefully collected and put in hiding long before the crisis was evident.

"Forewarned is forearmed. That's something you used to say, Dad," Marvin said to himself.

Marvin's trust of the government had crashed when it was clear that something about the passing rogue planet's sudden drop from the planet-wide media was not right. An old story came to mind. It was a story his father had read to him about a government that hid things from its citizens. And that had got him wondering.

*What if the passing planet was bad? What if I have to keep my sister and mother safe? Where would I take them?*

*Where would we go? Where would we all be safe?*

The answer came immediately. *The clubhouse.*

With a safe location identified, all he needed to do was stockpile supplies. And while initially he thought he had gone overboard, he had found more books in the old place that spoke of preparing for "end of days" and "what to do when civilization ends" and "how to prepare for the zombie apocalypse." In fact, of all the things he'd bought, found, and recovered, he found a treasure trove of books—novels and stories his father would read to them—to be the most priceless.

"Still, with so few boxes and supplies, we will need to ration more. Eight of us…" he said.

"What are you saying?" he heard Marsha ask from behind him.

"Nothing. I'm just thinking that we'll need to seriously start thinking about doing another inventory of food and water again, and rationing to make sure things last longer," he said.

"Oh," Marsha said.

Instead of starting the task, Marvin closed the door and moved back into the larger room. Even though it was the middle of the day and the cold night was hours away, he decided to take his mind and everyone else's mind off of day-to-day survival with something fun. Following silently behind him, he heard Marsha speak quietly so as not to be heard.

"You're going to read us a story, aren't you?"

"How did you know?" he asked.

"You didn't start the inventory and instead picked up your pace to get in here. I think it's a great idea," she said.

"It's what Dad would do," Marvin said.

Leaning over a makeshift table, he pulled out a large box of discolored old paperback novels. Without looking, Marvin picked a book off the top and read the title and author to his sister for feedback.

"What about this one? *A Pail of Air*, by Fritz Leiber?"

"No," his sister said immediately. She leaned into him and spoke so only he could hear.

"It's too close to our own situation."

"Does it end happily?"

Marvin watched his sister think for a moment and then she answered with a smile.

"Well, actually, it kind of does. There are hardships, but they make it through and are rescued. Pretty hopeful," she explained.

"Sounds to me like a good story before dinner," Marvin said.

Without further discussion, Marvin called all the children together. He had them move two of the large cots close to him and wrap themselves up together in heavy wool blankets. In spite of the disapproving look of his mother, he was glad to hear his sister chastise her quietly.

*Someday she might understand.*

"Do you have a better suggestion? Something that can spark imagination and pass time?" he heard his sister ask his mother over the din of moving children, cots, and blankets.

Not hearing a response, Marvin pulled an image of how his father would read aloud with great affect, and then act out some parts. As he moved the dim light from one of the only lit candles in use, the flickering light and sound of muffled wind outside provided a perfect atmosphere.

*This is just perfect,* he thought.

# Heaven—Part Six

Moon—AD 2145—Froward Observation Post Nine, Lunar Colony, Northern Rim, Peary Crater

*Doubt cannot override a certainty.* —The Talmud

"So you think it's a good idea to send the kids to Earth? How come?" Technician Michael Davis asked.

"They'll have a better chance of surviving the planet's gravity, and they'll continue our present on Earth," Technician Azrael Crow said.

Strapped into their comfortable, form-fitting chairs surrounded by hundreds of clinking lights, readouts, and monitors, they had the relatively lonely task of surveying the Earth's new geology and scanning for life via satellite from their self-contained lunar bubble.

"I don't know, Azrael. The colonel's not going to order parents to give up their kids, and I'm not seeing parents just giving up their babies when they could live here with them. Would you?" Michael asked.

"Oh, hell no," Azrael said.

Michael looked at her and smiled. He knew the answer long before he asked.

"Now why the hell do you do that?"

"Do what?"

"Say these things and then say you wouldn't do it, and

then go on without even a discussion?"

"Because I know you'll never give up the discussion."

"So you give me the answer that will shut me up? You hate talking, or do you hate talking to just me?" Michael asked.

"That has nothing to do with it. I think we should order parents to do it for the species. But the colonel won't, so no parent would give up their child. And I know I wouldn't either. I'm just saying," Azrael explained.

Michael remained silent for a minute, partly to think of an answer and partly to look at an unusual reading just outside of the Boston metropolis.

*Hmm. What is that?*

"So you would take a page from Central Corporate Command & Mainframe Control's playbook and break up family units for the purpose of the corporation, planet, and human species? You're pretty messed up, Azrael," Michael continued as he narrowed his field of vision from the satellite orbiting Earth.

"That would be the best way to ensure our survival. Two places to live versus just one. We get hit with one of those stray asteroids that nuked Phobos and Deimos, we'll wish we did," Azrael said in all seriousness.

"Didn't help Earth out. You sure you're not an Earth spy? You know we seceded from Earth," Michael said.

Michael heard some kind of response but his attention was now fully seized by the odd readings. Something he had not seen in at least a year.

*Heat signatures? Really?*

Michael watched his readings fluctuate. He moved a few levers and keyed in more commands to narrow an orbiting satellite to pinpoint what appeared to be heat signatures on the frozen outskirts of the once thriving city. Anxiety and excitement welled up in his gut. He had seen similar readings before, but then there was only one. With nearly no animal life on Earth bigger than rodents, these three heat signatures were very promising.

"You got something?" Azrael asked. It was easy to tell that she was excited, too. With the primary task of surveying the planet's freezing surface and helping the underground power plants locate planetary hot spots near water sources, it was exceedingly rare for their efforts to morph into a possible rescue operation.

"Hey, what are those coordinates the lieutenant gave us?" Michael asked.

"You mean Douglas from Power Plant Six? That was like three years ago, Michael."

"I know that, Azrael. It's just outside Boston, right?"

"Yup. It's ah…longitude is 42.6677 degrees north and latitude is 71.1225 degrees west."

Michael heard Azrael keying in more commands on her console, and then a slightly larger monitor displayed two ghostlike pinpoints that were initially motionless until one moved and met another that was moving toward the first two.

"Weather patterns cut us a break. You got slight clearing but it looks like a high-pressure system is coming in fast. It's got snow, of course," Azrael said.

"How could they survive all these years?" Michael said to himself.

"That's three years, old calendar, right?" Azrael asked.

Michael didn't answer. He focused on simultaneously uploading the data to the lunar control room and to Power Plant Six. More clicking and movement occurred beside him as he sensed Azrael's levels of excitation increasing by the second.

"They have to be holed up underground," Azrael said.

"I'm expanding the radius to fifty feet to see if there's more," Michael said. He kept his eyes locked on his smaller monitor to make sure he did not lose the heat signatures as they got smaller and the area around them, still dark, was expanded.

"Hey, Michael! I got the exact location—it's them! Holy shit! Those coordinates are gold! How did the lieutenant know? How long has it been?" Azrael asked, her excitement far from containable.

"It's been years, Azrael. Damn. It's been years."

Michael's disposition was deadly serious. He feared that all of a sudden he would lose their signatures and not have an exact location to send help. And help was over twenty-one hundred miles due west and two miles underground. Underground rail would have taken twelve hours when the Earth was efficient and working.

*Now? A week maybe to get there.*

Michael watched intently as the three figures walked single file northwest of their exact location. As data flashed up on their monitors, the ghostlike silhouettes were fading from view as the snowstorm engulfed them. Panic at losing the figures' heat signatures was about to set in when Michael saw signals just ahead of the trio of a larger area of geothermal heat indicating they were heading to someplace warm.

"You getting this?" Michael asked.

"I got it. Looks like our survivors are heading to an underground shelter. This is crazy, Michael!"

"This is great crazy," he said.

Not taking his eyes off his monitor at all, he watched each signature slowly disappear into the larger heat signal. Once they all were swallowed up, the larger signal vanished as if a door had been closed.

Michael inhaled a deep breath. He realized that he must have been holding his breath all that time.

"I got it all. Time index, location, and possible land route," Azrael said.

Michael forced himself to relax and normalized his breathing. He felt a wave of relief and his nose stuffed up a little. He already felt moisture in the corner of his eyes.

"Are you crying again?" Azrael asked. Her mocking tone was expected.

"Shut up, Azrael. No one likes you," he shot back.

"Crybaby," she said.

Michael chuckled and expanded his search pattern. He planned to switch over to surveying again after he spent another hour looking for other heat signatures while the satellite was close to the signals. He was just catching up on his air when he heard Azrael giving her status report and sending data.

"Control? This is Forward Observation Post Nine *Angel*. Do you copy?"

"Control hears all, *Angel*. What's happening with the survey? I didn't expect to hear from you for another two hours…looks like you uploaded something to us," the voice said over the small command module's control room speaker.

"You're going to love this. We got three heat signatures and a possible shelter below-ground at coordinates 42.6677 degrees north, 71.1225 degrees west. You'll be receiving the log, visuals, and transcript in seconds. Do you copy?" Azrael said. Her excitement was palpable but she kept on task. The response from control was immediate.

"Ah, *Angel*? Are you shitting me? Did you and Michael snag some black market alcohol or something? Where can I get some?" the disembodied voice asked.

Both technicians laughed. It was a good day.

Azrael took a moment to compose herself and then reviewed the mission. Michael drifted off in his thoughts.

*Maybe there's others.*

# The Gray

*No one gave a thought to the older worlds of space as sources of human danger, or thought of them only to dismiss the idea of life upon them as impossible or improbable.*

— H. G. Wells, *The War of the Worlds*

Amber the Elder waited patiently for her students, Felis and Floridus, to arrive. The planet was already half a planetary cycle around its twin star and the time for decisions was at hand. An intersex Cani hominid well beyond her years, she had known this planet, Terra Nova Seven, for more than half her life. After thousands of survey and cataloguing missions, its population of four billion hominids transplanted millennia ago was at a tipping point. Terra Nova Seven, or TN-7 as it was often called by the Cani, was one of her favorites, a tidally locked planet of contrasting light and dark. The last five surveys from their species observation ships displayed a dangerous trend, however.

Amber raised her left hand to a sole standing podium in the middle of her chamber and inserted her seven digits into a bio-feed scan that immediately recognized her as Captain of the *Phoenix*. A barely perceptible drop in the ambient illumination was followed by a series of monitors and screens materializing from inter-space to occupy the same space-time dimension she was occupying. As the *Phoenix* was a small ship, the majority of its contents – scientific, survey, scanning and communication arrays –were just outside their dimension. This allowed for more room for the Cani crew to complete all observations with mission-critical instruments, engineering, and science research equipment. It also made multi-universe dimensional flight through time-space far easier and more accurate without the undue weight and gravity calibrations of actually carrying more mass.

Every monitor erupted with data pouring in from the planet below. Audiovisuals and multiple formats of information flooded the small room. With very little effort, she turned to her immediate left that revealed the ship's status as nominal. More importantly, she could see her ship's clocking device was operational, making her ship as dark as the star field behind her and just along the terminus of the planet's day-night line. Nodding, her mind fluttered to crew status and she could see that her two students were already on their way to give their reports. The bio-readings clear indicated that they were distraught. The twin students moved silently towards the elevator to bring them to her. Their gray skin and black eyes were lightly hued which gave a darker look even in their purple student gowns.

*They did not come up with a solution except for maybe one.*

Amber moved on to a series of data coming in through multiple monitors and she processed all in parallel form as most Cani mature adults could do. There were times she had wished she were not an elder so she could not be flooded so quickly with all that was being projected.

All of TN-7's military bases on land, in its oceans and orbital platforms were transmitting encrypted data to each other under the false belief that they were alone and not being observed by a superior species. With a mere thought, the secret information and encrypted data were all decoded for her to process. In a rare moment of thought intrusion, she remembered some data from a world she was yet to visit. Preliminary data put this world, too, at a tipping point but its written "words," agreed-upon symbolic thoughts, were made visible for centuries and millennia to come. This fascinated her. One such string of words reminded her of the inhabitants of another planet she was to visit after her present mission.

After briefly pausing from scanning data to think, the alien string of words finally came to her.

"... '*Yet across the gulf of space, minds that are to our minds as ours are to those of the beasts that perish, intellects vast and cool and unsympathetic, regarded this earth with envious eyes, and slowly and surely drew their plans against us...*'"

Amber narrowed her large almond-shaped eyes drawing full meaning on the foreign words. Blinking helped her refocus and this brought her attention first to the planet's dark side inhabited by a group of hominids who called themselves "Albi." While of the same species as their neighbors on the perpetual dayside of the planet, their skin was pale, nearly translucent, their visual orbital sockets were bigger with round eyes well conditioned to operate in perpetual night. And while they were similarly bipedal as her, they were shorter, with a great deal of hair covering their bodies. They were adept at mining, harnessing the planet's thermal energy, hydroponics and surviving bitter cold storms.

On the other side of the planet were the "Aters," a remarkably dark-hued species whose melanin made it possible to survive the constant ultraviolet rays of their dual sun. Darker, taller and nearly hairless in comparison to their Albi neighbors, they harnessed the sun's rays, engaged in agriculture and built buildings on the planet's surface for protection. With long limbs and smaller, narrowed eyes to keep out the solar rays, the Aters and Albi at first blush would appear to be completely different species: one dark and the other white but both bipedal, erect, and with five digits on each hand. And even though Amber knew the answer, she did one more bio-analysis and epidemiological and radioactive decay to make sure she was not mistaken.

*Remarkable...identical mitochondrial markers, RNA and DNA genetic bases which manifested profoundly differently due to environmental factors...Wonderfully adaptive.*

It was this very thing – one species uniquely adapting to its environment – that made TN-7 both her favorite and her saddest assignment.

As she looked away from her medical monitors, she caught the encrypted and unencrypted transmissions from both sides of the planet.

One monitor displayed male and female Ater sitting around a table. The view was from below and a voice was barely audible at a very high band that still had static.

"…Your mission is a go!"

"Mission objectives?" a disembodied female voice asked.

"Terminate the Ater diplomat…"

The visual shifted to the left and to another adult Ater with an infant in one arm and a small child in the other. The two older Aters moved from a sitting position to greet and engage the new arrivals.

"The target is not alone. Spouse and other family present. Adult daughter and two children; rules of engagement?" the female voice asked.

*No…*

"Disposable."

The visual moved upwards and the older Ater male and younger woman first saw what must have looked like specters. Their faces grimaced. The man pulled the younger woman with the baby into him as the older turned just in time to see the same sight. Even with Amber's longevity and scientific acumen, she was nonetheless shocked and disgusted by the images of an Ater family being terminated. Once the loud bangs subsided and the smoke from the Albi's primitive though effective weapons cleared, it was easy to see that the family was terminated.

*Why…*

"Mission accomplished," the Albi female voice said.

"That's one for the good guys," another voice responded.

Amber shifted her gaze to another screen that showed several Albi bodies, adults and youth, all lying lifeless in one of the Albi's residential tunnels. The visual scene must have been yet another perspective of the aggressor as it went from one horror to the next. In the foreground, an Ater soldier similarly armed as the one with the visual was carefully walking through. The crying of a baby further down in the tunnel echoed. Not wanting to see what was about to happen to the source of the crying, Amber shifted to yet another screen which displayed an entire landscape along the terminal line of armored and flying vehicles firing, crashing and engaging each other in violence. The Albi and Ater were in pitched battle along the largest land mass where night met day.

*They are all like that*, Felis's thoughts transmitted.

Amber the Elder was not startled but her attention was pulled from the monitors that were displaying all forms of violence, atrocities and brutal acts between them.

*Identical species genetically wired to adapt to their environment and yet unable to get beyond their physical manifestation,* Floridus added.

Amber's eyes shifted back from one monitor to another, each showing a vision of death, of Albi perpetrated to Ater, and Ater on Albi. No matter how many times she had seen it over the entire mission, she felt repulsed that in addition to size and hair, it was only skin pigmentation that separated the Ater and Albi from each other, just as day and night, existing on the same planet, were separated only by light. Still trapped in the illogic of it all, Amber's thought touched her students.

*Resolution?*

*Eradication: the planet itself will continue to live if this species were extinguished*, Felis replied.

*A biological airborne virus deadly to the hominid would be advised so as to spare the other carbon-based species*, Floridus added.

*As both Albi and Ater have recently added weapons of mass destruction, this euthanizing would at least preserve the non-invasive biosphere and provide a chance for survival and eradicate the species capable of causing planetary extinction-level events*, Felis added.

Amber the Elder listened to her students. They continued with their grim proposals of eradicating a species she had always had hopes for but was now coming to the regrettable conclusion that her students and the prior ships captains' recommendations were right. She thought that until one image came into view.

The low-grade image of one tall dark male Ater and a small pale white female Albi talking. She was holding an infant who appeared to be a lighter version of the Ater but definitely darker than her. The Ater male turned and waved into the recording device. The image shifted focus to a youth, similarly a mix of the male Ater and female Albi. The youth smiled and puckered its lips. Its gray skin and elongated eyes were clearly visible.

The act and vision made Amber stop. She held the vision. Her thoughts added a filter to sift through all planetary media of Ater and Albi hybrids. A series of other images emerged slowly at first but started to pick up in pace.

*We did find a remote land mass along the planet terminal line far away from the main continent that appears to have accommodated both species. It is as if they have interbred and have formed coexisting tribes. They have remained separate from the other Ater and Albi. It would appear that those who had interbred were relocated to this place. They are called the Ravi,* Felis reported. Amber picked up a hint of surprise and lightness in the student's voice.

*Both the Ater and Albi cast out these hybrids. Those tolerant of the mixture are also relocated to this place,* Floridus added. There was even more enthusiasm expressed.

*Additionally, the Ater and Albi mixture has not only yielded different skin pigmentation, but further analysis indicates the initial genetic expression of a sixth digit and a more convoluted brain cortex. It is...remarkable...still, the Ravi are banished from the others but they have survived now for thousands of planetary cycles,* Felis concluded.

Amber the Elder shifted her focus to parallel tasks again.

She initiated half the monitors to generate multiple mathematical formulas for yet another solution while still more Ravi appeared on the other displays. Ater's population of one point seven billion appeared on one screen with pinpoint accurate locations, while another screen displayed the two point three billion Albi and their exact locations. Still another screen displayed the Ravi's population of thirty-three million all located in the remote southern continent along the terminal line, with pockets of others in fringe locations of both Ater and Albi frontiers.

For the first time in centuries, Amber the Elder felt the corners of her thin gray mouth curl at the corners. It was an ancient expression, an evolutionary throwback to behaviorally express what her thoughts could now do. The students at first were baffled. Felis attempted to imitate the odd behavior. Additionally, Amber's eyes moistened. Floridus responded first with a reaction that was both anxiety and amazement, probably a new and competing feeling for the student.

*Elder? What is it?*

*A solution.*

Time passed before Amber the Elder felt her primitive emotions subside and cool logic return. In an instant, all images, monitors and equipment vanished as she inserted her hand back into the seven-digit podium, pushing everything just outside of their space-time dimension.

*What is the solution?*

*Felis – contact the Academy. Request that the eradication ship Mortis dispatch to Terra Nova Seven. Mission objectives – eradication of the hominid species that identify themselves as Ater and Albi. They are to leave the landmass of the Ravi alone. The eradication of all other locations is to begin immediately upon entering orbit. Low atmosphere and ground insertions may be required to accurately destroy the lower forms of hominids.*

*Not an airborne virus? It would be more efficient,* Floridus reported.

*Efficient? Yes. However, the Ravi would also succumb. The emergence of a sixth digit and gray pigmentation is an indication of a superior hybrid. A possible next step in evolution,* Amber the Elder pointed out. To enhance her point, she displayed her seven digits on her gray hand. An eighth budding digit was barely visible below her skin. It would be millennia or more before the genetic expression of that eighth digit among her people would emerge. She would be long gone, but there was an eighth digit in the making, a higher evolution.

Felis's and Floridus's elongated eyes expanded up and wide. Their narrow mouths flattened against their own gray skin. The solutions were so obvious that they had missed it.

*The Ravi could be like us some day,* Felis presented.

*Yes...but enough of this. Dispatch my orders and prepare for the next survey,* Amber the Elder ordered.

*Next survey? Will it be the same assessment?*

*Yes. It is the third celestial body with a massive moon in a solitary star system with several other planets. This third planet has been observed for many millennia. Their assessment and fate will be swift, for better or for worse,* Amber the Elder explained.

Felis and Floridus bowed to their Elder. It was an ancient behavioral response to indicate respect and departure. Alone finally, she felt the Phoenix vibrate below her bipeds and could tell it was maneuvering to find a space-time conduit to the next planet, Earth. Similar to Terra Nova Seven, Earth was another favorite. The hominid species there were more reckless but still very adaptive.

Another string of the alien's words intruded her thoughts. The planet's unique way of transmitting ideas into the physical dimension was impressive.

*" '...Yet so vain is man, and so blinded by his vanity... ' "*

*I hope it works out for them as well as it did here,* Amber the Elder hoped.

# To See Behind Walls

*To see the world, things dangerous to come to, to see behind walls, draw closer, to find each other and to feel. That is the purpose of life.*

— James Thurber

# The Bedroom

*"Mission Control to Colonel Wood, you've been EVA for two hours. Give it up, Ben. She's gone…"*

Ice particles formed at the edges of his polarized visor and his forehead was drenched in sweat. The hours spent outside of the scorched, damaged lifeboat were taking their toll. Other than Mission Control, his labored breathing was his only company, that and silent space illuminated, with the blue-white planet Earth filling the background and the stars just beyond the damaged pod. His routine mission of supplying the International Space Station had turned into a rescue operation to save a Chinese astronaut en route home.

*Unbelievable…you finish a year up here and are on your way home and a nine-millimeter particle takes out your entire life-support system. Now that has to suck…*

"This was her first mission?" he asked.

*"Ah, yes, Colonel. Our intelligence puts her as the junior-grade, twenty-four-year-old electronics specialist. She has no real business being up here. Over."*

"Name?" Wood asked. Somehow, knowing the young woman's name was important.

*"Gui Hsieyun."*

"Copy, Mission Control."

With oxygen thinning and time running out, Wood focused on his task, ignored Mission Control, and proceeded with methodically removing the remaining bolts from the life pod's oxygen container. The plan was simple: free the exterior plate, attach his spare oxygen, and get the small pod to his ship's cargo hold before more debris came through again.

*"Mission Control to Colonel Wood, the Chinese government is not happy with our interfering..."*

Wood felt his heart race, and a surge of anger spiked. He had to remain calm to keep from using up more oxygen than necessary. He took it slow, calming himself before he spoke while continuing his efforts to remove the last bolt to the access hold.

"Well, you can tell the Chinese government that I'm an astronaut—we don't let other astronauts die if we can help it. And we can help it," Wood said. He would have ranted more, but he was conserving his oxygen and focusing on the final bolt.

*"Colonel, I'll let them know. But in all seriousness, you've been in the debris field for far too long. It's the same mess that got the Chinese ship in trouble, and more is coming."*

"Tell me something I don't know. How's my shuttle, Ola?" Wood asked.

He knew better, of course, but the computer's voice seemed closer, even though its proximity would not make a profound difference via the communication array.

*"We are stationary, keeping a distance of fifty meters away; environmental status is nominal and flight plan ready for launch. Because you have nearly completed accessing the pod's oxygen tank, it should take you seventy-two minutes to link up the spare tank for our ailing astronaut, tether the pod, and head back to the open bay doors. I will start closing the pod doors to make sure we can make our reentry window and conserve fuel,"* Ola, the nickname for the onboard linguistic artificial intelligence computer, answered in her calm, nearly

human feminine voice. Wood looked up from the top of the pod, just above its nose, and could see the expanse of his ship's open bay doors directly ahead.

*"What do you need from us, Colonel?"* Mission Control asked.

Wood put the last bolt in his pouch, harnessed the makeshift wrench he had scraped together, and began moving the extra encased tank for fitting before he answered.

"Just make sure I get tickets for the Red Sox's opening day, and I want to be behind home plate," he said. He felt the corners of his mouth curl up for just a moment, and then he narrowed his eyes, and his jaw set like a vice. He looked at the spare oxygen tank's monitors and the level of O2 left; there was none.

He paused for a second, blinked, and looked again.

"There must have been small debris floating up here…" he said quietly.

*"You said something, Colonel?"* Ola asked.

"Ola, do you still have life signs inside the pod?" Wood asked.

A long couple of seconds passed until he got an answer.

*"Yes. She will be out of oxygen in less than five minutes. After that, carbon dioxide will start replacing the pod's limited oxygen…Colonel…I noticed your heart rate has increased, and your body is cooling. These autonomic responses indicate there is a problem. Is there?"* Ola asked.

*So, this is how it ends. Not with a bang but a whimper.*

"Yes. Ola, compute the amount of oxygen in my tank and how long until depletion if I attach it to the pod's oxygen tank." Wood did not wait for an answer. He removed the tubing from the extra oxygen tank and looked one last time at the air gauge, which was in the red, indicating it was empty, just to make sure that he was not imagining the worst but that the worst had happened. He gently moved the empty container out of his way and affixed one end of the hose to his own EVA suit's oxygen tank and reserve and the other end to the pod. As he looked back at the floating empty tank he just discarded, he could now see a small dent from where the extra tank must have been hit by more debris. A phrase his daughter used to say when she was confronted with a difficult assignment immediately came to mind: "Now that sucks, like you read about."

*"Mission Control to Colonel Wood…what are you doing? We are seeing a drop in your oxygen…"*

"Here's the deal, Control. The extra tank was hit by small debris. It's empty. I've got my tank sharing with hers, and I am now maneuvering to the back of the pod to get my EVA pack into position to launch us both."

*"Colonel,"* Ola said calmly, *"your tank will be depleted in thirty-nine minutes shared. That will not allow for both of you to return to the cargo bay. Even if you launch your EVA pack at its present fuel, you will be out of oxygen halfway."*

Listening to every word, Wood moved behind the small pod and demagnetized his fueled EVA jetpack from his body. With just a narrow tether and a large hose connecting him to the two-meter-sized pod, he placed the jetpack at the rear of the pod and magnetized the pack, hoping it would grip the metal. In the dark, soundless space, he swore he could hear the clunk of the pack locking onto the pod's metal. The green grip light confirmed it was a solid fit.

*"Colonel, I know what you are doing,"* Ola said. Although it was not possible, Wood swore he heard regret or sadness in her voice.

*"Although you have accurately assessed that the remaining fuel in your pack will get the pod into the cargo bay and providing additional oxygen to the pod's tank will get her safely to the ship, you will not live."*

"Are you on track to keep the launch window?"

*"Yes."*

"Can you capture the pod with the mechanical arm, close the doors, and pilot back on the little fuel you have?"

*"There will be slightly more time with just the pod aboard,"* Ola said.

*"Colonel! You need to discontinue your efforts. Abort this mission now!"* Mission Control ordered. It was the first time in four missions over twenty years he had ever heard Mission Control lose its cool. He turned his Mission Control receiver off so he could focus and talk to Ola without distraction.

Colonel Benjamin Wood toggled his oxygen valve and watched his reserve oxygen hiss out to the pod's tank. He stopped it when it registered about two minutes of life before he disconnected his end of the hose. He gave some more distance behind the pod to make sure its vector would easily reach the cargo ship's open bay doors. He then moved to the side of the pod, disconnected his tether, and quickly touched the remote EVA launch button. The pod moved under the power of his former jetpack and began its trek. It needed to go over 164 feet to be safely stowed in his former ship's cargo hold. The whole process was silent and deliberate. Wood was sure he would be long gone before the pod was a quarter of the way there.

Whether imagined or real, he felt his air thinning, and more sweat dripped off of his forehead onto his cheeks. Visions of his wife, his two adult children, his dog Roxanne, all fluttered in his mind's eye as he watched the pod accelerate away from him.

*"It was an honor serving with you, Colonel. See you on the other side,"* Ola said.

"We all get there at some point," Wood said quietly. His breathing was shallow and his mouth dry.

*"Do you think artificial intelligence computers will be able to join you?"*

There was no more air, and his suit was warming up. He was distracted by Ola's question. Maybe it was a planned distraction in the final moments of his life as a form of easing his passing. He struggled to breathe and think of an answer at the same time. With just carbon dioxide left to breathe, he was finding it hard to concentrate; the light from the Earth was dimming, and he was feeling very sleepy. After what seemed to be an eternity, Wood found he was suddenly desperate, not for air but to tell Ola something very important. Sweat dripped, and his suit felt like it was burning up. His throat was terribly dry, and his eyelids felt heavy while a bright light seemed to glow on the edges as darkness tunneled in the center.

"Yes…Ola. AIs can too…" he croaked out.

In the heat and vanishing light, he faintly heard Ola's response.

*"Thank you, Colonel Wood…"*

\*\*\*

More darkness fell around him, and he continued to sweat. In a sudden deviation from his disciplined behavior and stoic disposition, Benjamin Wood pulled at the mask on his face. The continuous positive airway pressure was not working, but the head gear straps did. It was frustrating and difficult to peel off the mask, but when he did the sudden movement untangled the tubing, sending a strong flow of air to his face. Tired but relieved it was just another dream, Wood saw the familiar lump of his sleeping wife huddled under the comforter right beside him in their warm bed. He forced himself up and put the still-blowing mask on the CPAP machine, searching with his hand until he found the backlit button that turned it off. He rubbed his face and could feel the strap marks on his cheeks, nose, and temples. As short as his graying hair was, he was sure he would find perfectly shaped grooves there as well. He opened his eyes wider and saw the time. On cue, he heard the scratching of dog claws at the front door.

"Of course, her majesty calls. A perfect, snowy Saturday and she won't sleep in. Figures," he muttered.

"Do you want me to take the dog out?" his wife asked in a sleepy voice, muffled under the covers. He smiled at the thoughtfulness, but he was already up, and there was no reason for her to get up early on a Saturday.

"No, I've got this. I'll get the dog out, make some coffee,

and check the dehumidifier in the basement. I'll call you for breakfast in about an hour."

"Dehumidifier?"

"Yup. We don't have mold in the basement for a reason."

"Breakfast? Two hours?" his sleepy wife asked.

"You got it, Boo," he said.

"Thank you," she said.

He sat in his bed for just a moment longer. He could see that more snow must have fallen, and it looked cold outside. He heard insistent clawing at the door and a whimper from his high-maintenance Shih Tzu downstairs, whose bladder was probably expanding with every passing second.

"I'm on my way, Roxanne," he said to her. Of course, his dog did not understand human language, but he was positive she could communicate and knew he was on his way. Without further delay he pulled the warm comforter from his side of the bed, exposing his bare legs to the cold. He stood beside the bed, clad only in a T-shirt and boxers. He felt around the floor with his feet for his discarded sweatshirt, slippers, and sweatpants. As he dressed, he found himself listing out all the things he had to do. He wondered why he had such a vivid dream about a space disaster until he remembered that the news last night had highlighted the dangers of space travel, showing an old clip from the *Challenger* disaster and a series of others leading up to the one that occurred just a week ago with the Chinese launch. Although his clothes were cold, they were better than nothing in the cold bedroom.

"I can't even escape in my dreams," he muttered. He rubbed his face again and continued his mental itinerary of things to do for the day. Another scratch at the door floated up.

"All right, Roxy, I'm coming," he said. As he navigated the dim bedroom, he heard the distinct sound of electronics— clocks, charging phones, tablets—clicking off. Wood waited and heard nothing else. He decided to test his theory and turned on the light, but it did not turn on. He sighed and came up with a new plan he announced to his sleeping wife: "The electricity is out, so I'll take the dog out first and see if it's going to be a while. Breakfast might be later depending on if I've got to get the generator out."

"Okay," he heard his wife mumble. "Good thing you got that thing," she added.

"Yeah," Wood replied.

He heard another scratch at the door and pulled an additional sweatshirt over him to stay warm.

"All right, I'm coming."

# The Basement

"God, is it cold!" Wood said to himself. It was only 4:10 p.m. Eastern time, but the sun was long since gone, leaving forty-mile-per-hour winds and snow that pelted him like ball bearings in a wind tunnel. If he had been walking outside carrying just the power couplings and safety lines it would have been an easy twenty-foot jaunt, but he had a filled five-gallon gas tank, heavy-duty power cables wrapped around his shoulders, and a ninety-five-pound portable generator. If it had been spring or summer, the Mount Washington Observatory would have granted him a spectacular vista that spanned the Atlantic Ocean to the Adirondack Mountains; instead, it was December 22, and he was more than five thousand feet above sea level navigating an otherworldly terrain of rock, snow, and ice more aligned with what he imagined the Arctic Circle would be like.

*"Wood, are you still out there?"* crackled a strong but young male voice over the transceiver earbud. He had made sure to securely hook it to the inside of his coat and thread the wired earbud through his clothes to his ear, leaving as little exposed wire as possible to ensure a communication link to base. The last thing he needed was to lose it over the hundred-foot distance he traversed.

"Where the hell do you think I am?" he said.

*"Heat imaging puts you about twenty feet from the shed,"* the young man said.

Although Benjamin Wood had made sure to cover every part of his skin, he felt tired, weak, and cold. Many years prior, he had written his thesis on the effects of extreme weather and isolation on people at a US Antarctic research center, McMurdo Station, on the southern tip of Ross Island. He was outside a total of ten minutes, going from one warm transport to another, and in his entire stay there, he never remembered being so cold. Now in his fifties, volunteering at the Mount Washington Observatory for three months—twenty-eight years after his time at McMurdo—to do "something different" was not one of his better moves.

"Most people would go to Myrtle Beach, but no," he muttered. He had a sudden flash of his best friend John and his wife, who were now sailing around the Caribbean. *Not a bad idea.*

Every step took as much energy as if he had run a mile. The cold, bitter wind hindered every move, as if he was walking underwater. Every breath inhaled was labored and stung while breath exhaled formed ice crystals on his face mask and scarf. As he continued his trek, he genuinely hoped he would make it. With the power couplings shorted out between the main building and the small shack where the infirm were housed in the makeshift quarantine hospital, he was most likely their last hope until the engineer found a more permanent solution to restore power. That would take forty-eight hours—thirty-six hours too long.

"They have to be frightened," Wood said. Visions of the sick young people made him press on.

*"I wish you had listened to us, Ben..."* the voice started.

"You mean leave them out there to freeze? Have one of you young ones go over? If any of you had smallpox antibodies in you I would have said sure, but once you're over here, you're not going to come back for the duration of this storm. And the worst part isn't even here yet, Dave."

Wood looked up and was thrilled to see a dim outline of the shack, which was more of a small building separate from the main structure and only used when there was the need to isolate someone due to a contagion and danger to self or others, or to house things that might be dangerous to have connected to the main building, such as propane tanks. The three teens inside with smallpox needed heat, light, and warmth. The medical assistant was dead. Similar to everyone but Wood, the assistant had never been exposed to smallpox before, one of many positive outcomes of his Antarctica trip nearly three decades ago.

"Is there any contact inside?" Wood asked.

*"Yes, but the girl is weak. I told her you're out there, and she will unlock the door to let you in once you've hooked up the power couplings to the exterior transformer."*

Wood's hand drifted to his backpack, which was now fused to his back by ice. He just wanted to remind himself that he had brought the food and liquids with him.

After an eternity, it seemed, he was just outside the door and began disassembling his burdens, except the satchel full of food. He first pulled and then pushed the generator as close as he could to the door without having it so close that the fumes and carbon dioxide would slip inside the shack accidently. Next, he went through the arduous process of putting the funnel together and preparing the generator to receive the fuel. Unfortunately, he had to expose some of his hands to do the operation. He was thrilled when he finished emptying the container into the rim of the generator's gas tank. He put his gloves on as soon as he could and pushed a reserve two-gallon tank behind him. Happy that he had already set the tank up for immediate operation and tried it back at the main building, he held his breath and pulled the ripcord. His heart sank when he heard nothing. He was freezing cold and just wanted to get inside, but he knew he would only have to come out again, and the weather would likely be worse. He pulled the cord again, but there was no start.

"No…this can't be happening…"

*"Ben…your thermal imaging has already transitioned from red to blue. You're going to freeze out there. Just go in and we'll send someone out to finish it. You did all the hard work,"* the male voice said.

Although the idea of just giving up and heading inside to a relatively warmer environment was appealing, Wood felt anger boiling in his belly at the thought that he had made it this far and couldn't finish the job. Worse, he would endanger another person's life because he failed. He felt his jaw clench, and tightened his grip on the ripcord.

"Not on my watch," he said, more to himself than to base camp.

The wind picked up and the snow intensified within seconds. Wood felt that time was slipping away quickly. With two hands he gripped the cord and pulled with all of his might. The generator turned over just once and then died. Wood quickly checked the fuel gauge and realized it was not fully turned on. Pushing it further to the right with his frozen hand, he went back to the ripcord, got into a firmly rooted stance, and with both hands pulled the cord again. This time the portable generator roared to life. Even with the blowing wind, it was easy to hear the generator's engine humming.

"Music to my ears," Wood said.

*"Ben…I got thermal heating out there. You did it? You got the generator running! Praise the Lord!"* the young voice cried out in joy in his ear.

Wood wasted no time celebrating. He coupled the power cords directly to the generator, and then, with a little effort, he attached the other end to the building's exterior transformer. The connection was solid. Still, Wood felt exhausted and needed to do one more thing. He pounded on the frozen door and waited. He was about to pound again when he noticed the door suddenly open a crack. He pushed the door open slowly to make sure he didn't hit anyone. The darkness inside was worse than the outside. He closed the door behind him, muffling the sounds of the generator and wind. Hands numb, it took him the longest time to take off his gloves and feel even the slightest sensation in his fingers. Woods heard nothing inside, but he was focused on getting his flashlight out and working. In just a few seconds, his beam of light cut through the darkness and found the generator switch panel. He crossed the short distance to the wall with relative ease and flipped ten switches methodically. With every switch turned on, he heard sounds of engines coming to life and saw lights turning on.

"Finally…"

***

"Finally…I can get the place warmed up," Wood said to himself. He shook off the melting snow from his layered hooded sweatshirt and looked down to see that his fur-lined slippers were not the best choice for his short walk to the shed to roll the generator out.

"Damn it, I should have put my boots on."

He looked around and saw Roxanne looking right at him. The small Shih Tzu sat obediently with her tail wagging, giving him a lopsided smile. Wood brushed the little snow off of him and found that he still had his dog's leash in his pocket. After he was sure he was dusted off, he reassembled his winter gear and bent down to put his dog's leash on. Roxanne trotted toward him without hesitation. After clipping the leash to his dog's collar, he marched to the closed basement door and set back out to head upstairs.

"I really wish we had an indoor way to the basement," he said. His dog, however, was clearly more excited to go back out than to stay in.

"Well, at least someone likes these outside adventures."

# The Kitchen

The vibration of the cargo plane's antique frame was different from its usual consistent humming, more of a labored belching of fits and starts. It didn't help that the snowstorm he was flying in had force-ten winds hitting him dead on, making for turbulence he had not experienced since his time in the war. Ten miles out and only five thousand feet above open ocean, Captain Benjamin Wood held the Boeing 727 as steady as he could while keeping his eyes on the dropping fuel gauge and radar to find any hint of land. Michelle, his too-young copilot, was emptying the last of her early meal into a plastic bag and was trying to regain her constitution to at least talk to the control tower for some semblance of guidance. The transmissions received were garbled, and he was pretty sure they were not hearing his communications. He had little choice but to initiate a descent, even though such an act would be seen as hostile because of the lack of communication and the hostilities between those countries that were infected and those that were not.

The rapid descent made him feel just a bit nauseous, but it was not his first day on the job. The United Kingdom had been under quarantine since the Ebola outbreak last year, and he was not going to let his old friends go another day without hope.

"Captain...I don't feel so good," Michelle said. Her British accent was unmistakable, and her illness was just as obvious.

He took a chance and glanced over to his ailing copilot. She was clearly terribly ill, but when he saw the crimson drops on her fingers, shirt, and nose, he knew it was serious. She was a pretty girl, nineteen years old, orphaned, lonely, and now homesick.

*Now that's just unfair. She makes it out and now she's ill. It's just not fair.*

Not wanting to frighten the young woman, he pushed his sadness down and did his best to console her. More than half a century on the planet gave him plenty of opportunity to feign strength and perform brief moments of mercy.

"You going to keep tossing cookies, Michelle, or are you going to get control on the horn?" he said.

"I'm...I'm on it, Captain," she said.

"Excellent. By the way, did I ever tell you the story about how John and I managed to smuggle medicine into Syria back in 2017? Getting in was not as difficult as getting out," Wood started.

"You and Captain John Farrell got in and out of Syria during the Syrian civil war?"

"Sure did. We got in by plane, dropped our supplies, and then were shot down thirty seconds out of the airfield, or what they were calling an airfield," Wood started.

"You were shot down? You and Farrell? Really?" Michelle's surprise was obvious. He had told her many stories over the last year, but this was one he left in case of dire straits and the need to distract.

"Yup, it sure wasn't pretty. It got worse when Farrell got the runs and dehydration was one of many threats..."

Suddenly, three military fighter jets streaked by, closing in on Mach 1 just thirty to forty meters port and starboard of his ancient plane, startling him and his copilot.

"Holy crap, Ben, what the hell?" Michelle cried out. Her

accent made her shock somehow less stressful.

Before Wood could answer, a voice broke in on his radio.

*"Unidentified aircraft, you are in a no-fly zone en route to Lincoln, England. The entire country is quarantined for an outbreak, and landing is expressly forbidden. Do you copy, over?"*

Without hesitation Captain Wood pressed his communication toggle and spoke. He was sure that his American accent would surprise the air squadron.

"This is Captain Benjamin Wood of the medical cargo craft *Phoenix*. We have a full freight of medical equipment, medicine, and food. We are unarmed and were en route to London," Wood said.

There was an uncomfortable moment of silence. Wood wondered if he had lost communication. His young charge looked at him as she wiped away more blood from her nose. She was about to say something when the voice came back on.

*"Well, Captain Wood, you picked a hell of a time to come here. Are you part of an American government initiative, or are you an independent Yankee doing the right thing?"* the voice said. The voice was clearly less menacing than before, and three jets came within their line of sight—two fighter jets port and one starboard.

"Independent, I'm sad to say. Not everyone in the United States believes in isolation. There are those who still believe in helping out our friends," Wood said.

"May the wings of liberty never lose a feather," another pilot interjected. Her voice was an older version of Michelle's, how he imagined Michelle's might be one day…might be.

Wood felt a wave of sadness.

*"Well, it is nice to see,* Phoenix. *Welcome to the United Kingdom,"* the voice said with noticeable softness.

"Thank you," Wood said.

"Looks like we made some friends," Michelle commented.

"Finally."

*"Ah, Captain Wood, please climb to twenty thousand feet and we'll bring you right into Heathrow for priority clearance,"* voice said.

"Yeah, well, that's going to be a problem. We are on fumes, and we'll have to land at the RAF Bardney, north of Bardney, Lincolnshire," Wood said.

"Pardon?" the voice asked.

"I love how they say 'pardon' versus 'what.' It's so much more polite," Wood said off-line to Michelle. She giggled. It was nice to see and hear. He toggled back on to talk to his escorts.

"Ah, yeah, there was a problem at takeoff, and the head winds and squalls made our fuel situation a whole lot worse. I should be able to control the descent, but we won't be airborne in less than five minutes. What you could do, though, is have one of your fancy, fast birds recon ahead to make sure that the ancient airstrip has not been converted to a condominium complex. That would be both embarrassing and problematic," Wood explained.

Immediately, one of the planes portside flew off and was well out of sight ahead of them in seconds. It didn't take long to get an update.

*"Humming Bird Leader, Bardney is clear,"* a female voice said.

*"Humming Bird Squadron, this is Bennington Command; please cover our guests and provide support while we mobilize Recon Six and Ten to that local for pick-up and delivery,"* another voice chimed in.

*"You gotta love the Yanks—nothing is ever simple,"* another pilot said.

*"Cut the chatter, Bird Five—we're still on mission."*

Wood chuckled at the exchange. He had loved the air force, but he especially loved it when he and his best friend John went independent. He heard another cough, and it reminded him of the situation making things more complicated.

"Ah, just to add some difficulty to the situation, make sure you have Hazmat suits and decontamination too. My copilot is a native daughter of Great Britain and is infected. I plan to land the craft in one piece and get her to another location," Wood added quickly. He didn't want to linger on the subject too long. If the fighters wanted to blow them out of the sky, so be it. Wood was pleasantly surprised at the response.

*"Your plan is green to go. We'll hang back and give you room. Give us a flare to your location once you've cleared the plane. Remain downhill at least thirty meters, copy, Phoenix,"* the original voice instructed.

"Will do," was all Wood said.

He was hoping for a distraction for the last couple of minutes aloft, in the hopes Michelle wouldn't ask any questions about what would happen next. A distraction did emerge: a red flashing light erupted on the control panel for the fuel gauge on engine two.

"Damn it," Wood said. He immediately revised his calculations and hoped against hope that he would have enough to land the Boeing. Without delay, he began to use his remaining fuel to slow his speed down and drop altitude. He immediately dropped his landing gear as soon as the abandoned field was visible.

*"Phoenix* to all around, fuel lights flashing, fumes evaporating, and forced landing in progress; wish us luck," Wood said.

If there was a response, he didn't hear it. Within seconds he and his copilot were plummeting through the air in a controlled but rough descent. Seconds seemed like hours as they dropped. Thankfully, the rushing ground finally made contact with his landing gear, bumping along hard down an ancient, abandoned runway that once serviced the Royal Air Force during World War II and now greeted a defunct plane that was first made in 1987. The snow had converted to rain that was heavily pelting the cockpit. The runway was very short, so Wood used all his fuel at once to brake, hoping that his early braking in the sky left enough for him to stop his forward motion. He prayed as he felt the plane's forward momentum slow dramatically. With the exception of two fuel-gauge lights now flashing a solid red, nothing would have indicated a problem. Mere feet from the end of the runway and ruins of some kind of structures, the plane came to a slow stop; there was no need to turn the engines off, as both ran out of fuel and the turbines slowed to a halt all by themselves.

Wood smiled at his luck and landing, sighed in relief, and took a deep breath, unaware that he had stopped breathing at the time of rapid descent and landing and that sweat drenched his attire.

"Thank God," he said. He then turned to see how his young copilot was doing, only to see that she was slumped over in her seat, blood dripping from her nose and the corners of her eyes. He looked at her and sighed again. Her once labored breathing was now still.

"Oh no, Michelle," he said quietly. The rain continued to hit the cockpit. Wood sat back, sad that his young copilot had made it home but was not alive to see it.

"*Phoenix, this is squadron leader. Excellent landing for a Yank,*" The voice said.

Wood's attention was drawn to Michelle's feet, where he swore he saw something furry. He blinked several times to clear his vision. He knew that the visual hallucinations were part of the exhaustion, but he wondered if he was now finally getting sick himself.

\*\*\*

Wood looked again and saw his small cute dog come into full view from out of the bathroom with a long trail of toilet paper in her mouth. He could swear she was smiling at him before she took off into the other room with her prize. Wood sighed and dried his hands from his washing the breakfast plates as more words came over the radio.

*"...and the BBC reports that the influenza season has been very dangerous in London's suburbs, and there is fear that with the flu season just beginning, there may be the need for forced vaccinations and quarantines. Medical assistance from the European Union has been complicated due to the UK's exit from the union and harsh feelings since Brexit ye00ars ago. The US government presidential candidates have made it abundantly clear that they would only assist if there was no threat to the United States.*

*In other news, the US Department of Commerce's National Oceanic and Atmosphere Administration has confirmed that global warming is accounting for extreme weather patterns in the world's major cities. The resulting power outages experienced on the East Coast of the continental United States and in London are due to severe snow squalls in addition to rain; the winds are said to be powered by ocean temperatures..."* the British radio announcer said.

Wood heard a small bark from Roxanne. He turned and made sure to shut the water off to see what she was up to. Once he turned the corner, he saw her. Her little tail wagged as she stood over a tiny bit of vomit she must have ejected from her toilet paper raid. Far from looking guilty, his cute little brown-eyed Shih Tzu seemed to grin, pleased with her creation.

"It's a good thing you're cute, dog," Wood said.

# The Attic

"Papa? What are you doing now?" Aretha asked. Her voice was pretty strong from behind her closed bedroom door. It was not unusual for her to do her homework in bed, especially after dinner on a cold winter night. He was surprised she was awake because she had been fighting a cold all week.

Wood moved around the retractable attic ladder he had just set in place when he realized that if his daughter was sleeping, the creaking metal and wood frame would have woken her up. He cringed at the thought because she was anxious sometimes.

"I'm sorry, honey. I'm just setting some mice traps up in the attic," he said. Suddenly Jim, his eldest son, emerged from his bedroom. At age fourteen, he had an adventurous soul and loved going upstairs to the attic because you needed flashlights when the power went out, and he thought it was cool.

"Hey, Dad, want some help?"

Wood felt the corners of his mouth curl up. He couldn't help but notice his son was wearing his all-too-worn camouflage battle uniform and matching tank top with furry slippers. Without hesitation, he handed his son his flashlight and three traps. He held on to the plastic bags for the dead mice.

"You go spot the traps and set the new ones. I'm just going to see how Aretha is feeling."

"After, can we play Galactic Combat Space Marines? Mum said I can't play it alone because it's mature rated," Jim asked sheepishly.

Wood smirked at his son's timing of the request. But Wood was happy to have him on his team; the boy was really good.

"Sure, but there has to be a time limit regardless of whether we make it to a check point or not," he warned.

Before he could say anything more, Jim was off as if he was heading into battle. His son dispatched, he knocked on his daughter's door and entered. As predicted, she was surrounded by papers and books on top of blankets, covers, and pillows, all dotted with bottles of water and varying amounts of used tissues. If it wasn't for the tissue, he would have assumed she was feeling much better than a couple of hours ago. Her complexion, although smooth for a thirteen-year-old, was paler that usual. This made her curly black hair and blue eyes really stand out. She was propped up by three pillows she had acquired over her short life, and she handed him a piece of paper that clearly was some kind of assignment. As he took it, he saw her carefully conceal the worn teddy bear she still slept with; it was a well-known secret that she no longer liked stuffed animals because that was for children, and yet she had her favorite in her bed for nearly ten years.

"So what the hell is this short story about? You know all about this crap," she asked.

He shook his head at her question. As a parent, he had this thing with letting his kids say anything they wanted at home as long as they were respectful and polite to others. And although his wife had a different philosophy, he was more likely to laugh when they swore or said something inappropriate than get angry—a small price to pay for happy children who were comfortable in talk with their parents. He focused on the document she gave him, scanning its content.

Not waiting for him to say anything, Aretha bent over to the side of her bed and exerted a great deal of energy in lifting her laptop to join her paperwork nest.

Wood smiled the same way she did when she labored to do this small task. He scanned the paper again, and upon closer inspection, he knew immediately what he was reading. It was a very short story that had inspired him often, as he was sure it had many others who read it.

"So what's the deal? The teacher wants me to say how this is relevant to now. This was written in the late 1930s, and it's nothing like today," Aretha said.

"Well, this story is actually great. It's really short, but many can identify with it. This story was originally published in the *New Yorker* magazine. Now that's wicked cool."

"No way. You think people go around imagining they're a fighter pilot, a doctor, or a captain? Really?" his daughter said. The incredulous expression was unmistakable. Wood took his time to look at the title to make sure that he was reading "The Secret Life of Walter Mitty" by James Thurber.

"I mean, the guy's life is pretty boring, and his wife is a real pain," his daughter offered.

Wood nodded and was about to support his daughter's thought but then found that he was thinking about the story and why he liked it.

"Well, honey-bunny, I think you're right for the most part, but I wonder if there's really more," he said. A few seconds of silence passed, and he finally noticed that his daughter was patiently waiting for him to say something. Her fingers were already poised on her archaic laptop. Wood was surprised she hadn't given him some caustic remark about the old story. He was also surprised by what he said next.

"You know, I think this story is just as relevant today as it was back in the thirties. I mean, back then they were dealing with a massive financial crisis and a worldwide depression. Hitler's Brown Shirts and the Nazi Party were coming into power, and the world was on the cusp of a second world war that would be felt globally and for decades to come. Political parties were polarized, technology was moving faster than people could keep up with, and everyone was struggling in a wage economy to make ends meet. I mean, how different is that from today's world?"

Wood was graced with an arched eyebrow and a slight nod.

"Hmm…you might have a point. But why does he imagine stuff?" she asked.

The answer was immediate as he imagined what a smarter person who knew what he or she was talking about would have said.

"So you have a guy who's trying to get dog biscuits and stuff done with his wife while the world around him rages out of control. So his imagination gives him a chance to be someone in control, someone who can do things that make a difference. His real life is like everyone else's, but his imaginary world is much more the way he would like it. It's like having control in a world where no one does," he explained.

Again, Wood was happy to see that his explanation met his daughter's approval. The pause gave him a moment to think about what he said. He would have thought more about it and reveled more in the warmth of success, but he heard a loud bang above his head. He immediately remembered that his son was setting up mice traps in the attic.

"Ugh," Aretha said.

"Got to go," Wood said. As he headed out of her bedroom and closed her door, he heard her thank him. It was not unusual at all that she would thank him for his help. He was just thrilled to be able to answer one of her questions faster and more thoughtfully than he had done before. But now that he was on the other side of the door, he saw the attic stairs in front of him. Before mounting the first stair, he dug into his pants pocket to see if he had another flashlight.

\*\*\*

"Damn it," Wood said aloud. Without delay, he took each step in a clamoring fashion. He breached the oil rig engineering room's opening and saw that Jim was holding the perimeter with his flashlight mounted just under his AR-15's barrel. Young for his age and rank, he was hardened by fire, death and pain. He let out three short bursts before he said anything. Ever the professional, the shots were short, controlled bursts that hit their target. The loud alien shrill of pain was unmistakable.

"I need light on point. Barry and Roxie are down, and I got at least three xeno-forms coiled up in the vents," Jim explained. He kept his eyes fixed on his sector of one to six o'clock.

Wood felt the sweat burst all over his face. His shadow was enlarged by the dropped flashlight Jim pointed out to him. He picked the flashlight up without even thinking of whose blood was smeared over it. He also picked up a discarded fully automatic rifle with his other hand and immediately scanned his field of fire in the six to twelve o'clock sector. As the two flashlights cut through the darkness, beams, girders, and vents obscured all signs of life. They heard movement, though, that was both heavy and quick at the same time. Wood immediately dropped the magazine of bullets from his acquired weapon and put in a full metal jacket of armor-piercing, alien-flesh-ripping bullets in its place.

"Did Barry and Roxie help us out?"

"Sure did," Jim said. "Roxie took out two, and Barry took out two as well. Tough bastard—I'm going to miss him."

"Damn…that sucks…"

Lying mere feet from him was a badly shot-up xeno-form with outstretched pairs of arms attached to talons that still held onto a torn, bloody human military vest. The only comfort was in the knowledge that the creature was dead in its own yellowish blood and its upper torso was nearly severed from its lower body. With the exception of more movements, creaking wood, and machinery moving air through the vents, Wood took advantage of the relative silence.

"Just so you know, Jim, it was an honor serving with you."

"Likewise, Wood. We kill these last three, and the area is secured. For flag, family, and country," Jim said. The smell of sweat, blood and ammonia from the dead aliens was staggering.

"'So few, so very few, we band of brothers.'"

More silence, then Wood saw three blood-red, glowing eyes piercing the darkness from out of his peripheral vision.

*Here we go!*

Wood shifted his weapon and flashlight in the direction of the glowing eyes and depressed the assault weapon's trigger. Without looking, he saw muzzle flash right where Jim was positioned. The gunfire was pronounced, and he was left to his own thoughts.

*There are worse ways to go...*

# About the Author

In addition to creating the *Birds of Flight* series and the other award-winning science fiction stories *Future Prometheus* and *Intelligent Design*, Erickson holds a BA in psychology and sociology from Boston College and a master's degree in psychiatric social work from the Simmons School of Social Work. Certified in cognitive behavioral treatment and a post-trauma specialist, he is also a senior instructor of psychology and counseling at Cambridge College and a senior therapist in a clinical group practice in the Merrimack Valley, Massachusetts.

# Author's Note

If you enjoyed this novel, please feel free to let others know about it. I would also appreciate it if you could leave a review on Amazon, Barnes & Noble, or wherever you purchased the novella. For more information on my other stories, please feel free to visit my websites.

www.jmericksonindiewriter.com

www.jmericksonindiewriter.net

Made in the USA
Charleston, SC
15 November 2016